READ ALL THE
SPY KIDS™
ADVENTURES!

COMING SOON!

Based on the characters
by Robert Rodriguez

Written by Elizabeth Lenhard

HYPERION
MIRAMAX BOOKS
New York

Text copyright © 2003 by Miramax Film Corp.
Spy Kids™ is a trademark and the exclusive property of Miramax Film Corp.
under license from Dimension Films, a division of Miramax Film Corp.
All rights reserved.

Printed in the United States of America

First Edition

3 5 7 9 10 8 6 4 .

This book is set in 13/17 New Baskerville.

ISBN 0-7868-1715-1

Visit www.spykids.com

CHAPTER 1

It was a sunny, summer afternoon, and Carmen and Juni Cortez were hard at work.

Homework, perhaps? Or baseball practice?

Not exactly. Their afternoon would be spent saving a major city from certain doom.

After all, that's the kind of thing that high-level, international spies do. Even if they are only ten and twelve years old.

Carmen and Juni were staking out a remote patch of land on the banks of the Stewhead River—the river that just happened to be the only source of freshwater for Stewston. Population: three million.

"My only question is, *Why* did Neiman Tode have to choose sturgleworms?" Carmen complained as she crouched next to her brother behind some scrubby plants. Both of them were wearing their spy gear—black cargo pants, utility belts for their spy gadgets, and black vests over high-tech, long-sleeved T-shirts bearing the logo "OSS." That stood for the Office of Strategic Services, which was the top-secret government organization that employed the Spy Kids.

"Because he's an evil madman," Juni said. "Who else would breed these disgusting creatures?"

Juni wasn't exaggerating. Of all the gross things in the world, sturgleworms were among the grossest. They were fat and greenish yellow. And any water they touched turned a puce color and started to smell like the sweatiest of locker rooms.

"It takes a pretty bad guy to infest an entire river with sturgleworms. That's why we've gotta stop Tode in his tracks."

"Stop me in my tracks?"

The Spy Kids froze.

They'd been staking out Neiman Tode.

But instead, he had found them.

"So . . ." Carmen said, glaring at Neiman Tode. "This is your secret underground lair. Say good-bye to it, Dr. Tode. You're going to be relocating."

Tode was dressed like the mad scientist he was. He wore a tattered, dirt-smeared lab coat. His rust-colored hair was coiled into dreadlocks that looked remarkably like slithery earthworms. And in his hands was an open box of sturgleworms.

Juni whipped a laser web blaster from his utility

belt and pointed it at the villain. One shot and Tode would be flailing within a net made of laser beams.

"Go ahead and shoot," Tode taunted. He was holding the box of sturgleworms with his fingertips. "But if you do, I'll drop my box of treasures here. And you know what that means. . . ."

"You're a sick man, Tode." Carmen spat.

"I prefer the term 'genius wormologist,'" Tode retorted.

Juni glanced at his sister. She returned his look and nodded, almost imperceptibly. Then Juni looked at Carmen's foot. She tapped her toe four times and cocked her ankle to the side.

That meant Maneuver Fourteen. The X ray. Juni nodded at Carmen and turned back to Tode.

"I don't know, Dr. Tode," he said casually. "I have a feeling this idea is gonna get squashed!"

Then, without a moment's hesitation, Juni pressed a button in his watch that activated the spring locks in the soles of his spy boots. The springs shot out, sending Juni flying through the air—straight toward Tode's ankles. He collided with the villain with a grunt, taking him down.

At the exact same moment, Carmen shot through the air, too. But she was heading for Tode's hands. The kids just missed each other, their pathways making an X in the air. Just as Juni smashed into Tode, Carmen plucked the box of sturgleworms from the evildoer's hands. She managed to keep the box upright as she somersaulted into a graceful landing. Then she swiped a liquid nitrogen aerosol from her utility belt and sprayed it into the box. Instantly, the worms froze.

"That won't hold them for long," Carmen muttered. "But hopefully, it'll last just long enough to get Tode in cuffs."

Setting the box on the sandy ground about ten feet from the river's edge, Carmen spun around to gauge Juni's location.

He was locked in hand-to-hand combat with Tode. And Juni was struggling, despite his OSS-honed martial arts skills. After all, Tode was twice Juni's size.

Carmen slipped one of her favorite gadgets—the Noosenick—out of her utility belt. When her trained eye detected the best moment for an offensive strike, she sprang to her feet.

"Juni," she said to the back of her brother's head. "Duck!"

Immediately, Juni crouched to the ground. Carmen aimed at Tode and deployed the

Noosenick. A long stretch of rope with a loop at the end shot out of the device. Carmen expertly maneuvered the noose over Tode's body. When the rope hit his waist, she yanked—hard! The noose tightened, pinning Tode's arms to his side. He toppled over, and his face hit Juni's feet with a gross, squelching noise. Tode was knocked out cold.

But there was one problem. A slight miscalculation in Carmen's brilliant rescue plan.

She'd forgotten about the unlocked springs in Juni's boots.

And when Tode's head hit the toes of Juni's boots, they flipped her brother off the ground like a tiddledywink.

"Aaaaaahhhh!" Juni yelled as he sailed through the air in a big arc.

"Juni!" Carmen screamed. "Watch out for the sturgle—"

Thwack!

That was the sound of Juni Cortez landing on the sandy river ground and skidding right into the box of sturgleworms.

Splooosh.

And that was the sound of five hundred disgusting, wiggling worms spilling out onto the ground.

Gush-gush-gush-gush.

And *that* was the sound of five hundred moist and smelly worms beginning to squirm their way toward the Stewhead River. Just as Carmen had expected, they had thawed out after a few minutes. In fact, they seemed even more energetic after their brief rest. If they hit the water, all was lost!

"We've got to contain the worms!" Carmen shouted as she watched Juni lurch woozily to his feet. He shook his head blearily.

Carmen began to run toward the writhing army of stinky worms. But she didn't get very far, because four hands suddenly grabbed her.

This, Carmen thought as she glanced at her captors, is *not* good.

She was in the clutches of two very strong and very mean adults—Tode's lab assistants and partners in crime.

The sturgleworms were only a few feet away from the Stewhead River.

And Carmen was *really* beginning to regret the conversation she'd had with her parents at the breakfast table that morning.

"Carmen, Juni," their father had said in his musical, Spanish accent, "I know this Neiman Tode interference is a Spy Kids mission. But maybe your mother and I should back you up."

"No, thanks," Carmen had said to Dad. "I think Juni and I can handle this one."

"Yeah," Juni said through a mouthful of Fooglie Puffs. The Spy Kids didn't like it when they needed backup.

So, *that's* why Carmen was now stranded in the clutches of crazed wormologists with no help.

"This had to happen on the *one* day we could use an extra pair of hands," Carmen muttered irritably. Then she started. What was that whooshing noise above her? Carmen looked up and gasped. She revised her plea.

"An extra pair of feet would be fine, too!"

Because that's exactly what Carmen saw—two feet clad in a familiar pair of black boots. They were attached to a girl decked out in OSS spy gear. She was harnessed to a cable that she'd rigged from a tree branch directly above Carmen and Tode's men. Her long, shimmering, brown hair flowed out behind her. And the soles of her boots were aimed like battering rams.

Carmen cringed and stiffened, bracing herself for a blow. But at the last minute, the girl thrust her feet out to either side, catching each thug directly in the chest and leaving Carmen untouched. While the shrieking villains sprawled into the dust, the mystery girl swooped over Carmen's head and released herself from her harness. She landed as lightly as a cat.

Carmen pulled her laser web blaster from her utility belt. She aimed at the dirt-smeared thugs and pushed the deployment button. Immediately, the men were caught up in a tangle of lasers. They kicked and flailed, but the virtual net had them tied up in knots.

Then Carmen turned to the new spy.

"Hullo," the girl said. She had an English accent. "Looked like you could use a spot of help."

Carmen was dying to know who this new spy was. But there was no time to make introductions now. They still had work to do. So, Carmen pulled two pairs of handcuffs from her belt.

"Thanks," she said to the girl, tossing her one of the pairs of cuffs. She pressed another button on her web blaster. The laser net immediately disappeared. But before the thugs could scramble away, Carmen grabbed one and slapped the handcuffs onto his wrists. The new Spy Kid quickly cuffed the other thug to his partner.

With the criminals taken care of, it was time to help Juni. He had pulled an expandable trowel from his gadget belt and was using it to scoop sturgleworms back into their box. But the worms had scattered across the riverbank by now. And some of them were squirming dangerously close to the water.

"My sturgleworms!"

At the sound of a man's voice behind her, Carmen jumped and spun around, her fists raised. But there was nobody there. Then she looked down and saw that Tode had woken up. He was still lying in the dirt, bound up by Carmen's Noosenick. He had a big, bruisey bump in the middle of his forehead from falling onto Juni's hard boot toes. But Tode didn't seem to care. Instead, he was gazing at the river. And he looked overjoyed.

"Sturgleworms!" he repeated, laughing. "You're almost there! Swim, my little wormies. Live free!"

"I don't think your worms are going to listen to you," the new Spy Kid said to Tode with a smirk.

With that, the girl pulled a small, red box from her utility belt.

"Let's see, I believe a frequency of eight twenty-five to the tenth power is just the ticket for paralyzing sturgleworms," the girl said. "Right, Carmen?"

Carmen slapped her forehead.

"Of course," she sputtered. "I totally forgot about the effect of superfrequency noise on gelatinous invertebrates."

"No!" Tode cried. "Don't do it!"

He wiggled around in the dirt, trying to scoot over to the girl. But she just laughed and flicked a switch on her high-frequency pitch device.

Immediately, the worms froze. As Neiman Tode screeched in protest, Carmen and the girl grinned at each other. The crisis was totally averted. Juni walked over with his eyebrows raised. The stranger smiled at him, too. Then she introduced herself.

"I'm Maya Sinclair. From the London branch of the OSS," she said. "And you're Carmen and Juni Cortez. Pleased to meet you. I'd just arrived at OSS headquarters when our satellites picked up on your troublesome situation here. They sent me out to back you up immediately."

Both Carmen and Juni hung their heads. They *really* hated it when they needed backup.

"Don't worry about it," Maya said quietly to Carmen. "After all, the intel indicated no need for backup. Even a level-one adult spy would have been in a fix with these three."

Carmen shot a grateful smile at the new girl. Then she nodded at the cuffed criminals.

"Why don't you radio for the OSS helicopter, Maya," she said. "We'll deal with . . . the worms. C'mon, Juni."

Carmen pulled out her own trowel and headed over to the paralyzed worms. But instead of helping Carmen trash the worms, Juni approached Maya.

"Hey, can I check out your high-frequency pitch device?" Juni was saying. "Looks like you have a more recent model than we have."

"Juni!" Carmen called again. "Get over here."

"In a *min*-ute," Juni called out to her as Maya handed him her little red box.

Juni squinted at the little box with a grin. He loved new gadgets. He gave the dial a little spin. And another spin.

Carmen's eyes widened. Suddenly, she remembered another fact about high frequency's effect on gelatinous invertebrates.

A very important fact.

Feeling as if she were moving in slow motion, she tried to call out to Juni. But before she could form any words, Juni spun the dial once more.

And that's when it happened.

KER-PLOOOOOWWW!

"Aaaaaaaaahhhhh!" Carmen, Juni, and Maya screamed.

"Noooooooooo!" Tode cried.

"Grooossssss!" The thugs bellowed.

When the noise died away, Carmen looked

down at her spy uniform. It was drenched in slithery, slimy, sturgleworm guts.

She glared at her brother, who was dripping with slime himself. She stomped over and grabbed the high-frequency device away from him. She stuffed it into her vest pocket. Then she asked Juni through gritted teeth, "Don't you remember this morning's OSS briefing?"

"The one where they said frequencies of a thousand or more will make sturgleworms explode?" Juni said. He cringed and shrugged sheepishly at his enraged sister. "I do now."

Before Carmen could yell at Juni some more, a thunderous noise filled the air. The kids were battered by a tremendous gust of wind.

They looked up to see an OSS helicopter bearing down on them. It had arrived to take the criminals into custody.

"Well," Maya said, walking over to Carmen and laying a gooey hand on her shoulder. "On the bright side, I think we can say the day is officially saved."

CHAPTER 2

After the OSS pilots had hauled Tode and his minions into the helicopter and taken off, Carmen, Juni, and Maya were left on the riverbank to pack up their gear and hit the road themselves. Juni pulled out a bag of Cheez Curls and began munching loudly.

"I've got an OSS car and driver waiting for me at Checkpoint Number Thirteen," Maya said, smearing some goo off her watch to access a map. "C'mon, I'll give you a lift."

"That's okay," Carmen said. She felt a little awkward. "We've got our jet packs." She pointed at the hydrogen-fueled backpacks she and Juni had used to fly to the Stewhead River.

"Oh," Maya said. She shrugged and looked a little disappointed.

Juni tried flicking his now-empty Cheez Curls bag off his hand. But it was stuck to his palm. The glue? Sticky sturgleworm guts.

"Ugh!" Juni said. "I need a shower, ASAP."

"That makes three of us," Maya said, flicking a gob of goo off her arm.

"You're right," Carmen said. "Maya, why don't you come home with us? You can take a shower, we'll have something to eat, and you can tell us all about the OSS-London."

"*Only* if you tell me about the X-ray maneuver," Maya replied with a grin.

"Which will *only* happen if we get going," Juni said, grabbing his gear bag. "C'mon, I stink!"

"I guess we'll take that ride, after all," Carmen said to Maya with a grin.

A short while later, Carmen, Juni, and Maya were sprawled in the Cortezes' big, Spanish-tiled kitchen. Their hair was freshly shampooed, and they were all wearing clean clothes. Maya had borrowed some jeans and a T-shirt from Carmen.

"I love the way your cook-bot does hamburgers," Maya said. She took a big bite of the dinner their kitchen robot had just made for them.

"Yeah, the burgers are good," Juni said, digging into his own custom-made food. "But you should really try this Hot Dog Surprise. You don't know what you're missing."

"Trust me," Carmen confided to Maya, "you don't *want* to know. I swear, one of our uncle's crazy inventions must have killed my brother's taste buds."

"Your uncle?" Maya asked politely as Juni (not so politely) stuck out his tongue at Carmen. It was bright green. Clearly, that was the "surprise" in the Hot Dog Surprise.

"Our Uncle Machete," Carmen said, pausing to take a bite of her black-bean burrito. "He's a great inventor. Well, except sometimes we get stuff before it's quite ready. So, you have laser guns that shoot bubbles, or vehicles that go in circles, or exploding gum that tastes like pimientos instead of peppermint—you name it."

"Except we *can't* name it," Juni said quietly, shooting his sister a look. Then he turned to their guest. "No offense, Maya, but Uncle Machete's gadgets are kind of a Cortez secret."

"Of course," Maya replied. She then turned to face Carmen. "Have you seen the new superwick textiles in the OSS line?" Maya asked. "Not only do they scramble sonar signals and become flotation devices in water—they also come in the coolest lavender color!"

"No way!" Carmen breathed.

"Of course!" Maya replied.

15

Juni rolled his eyes.

Why is Carmen acting like such a girly-girl? he wondered. But before Juni could say anything a voice stopped him.

"Hel-lo, Juni!"

Juni heard a very familiar, grown-up voice behind him. He spun around.

There was Mom, leaning against the kitchen door. Dad was right behind her, smiling at Juni.

Maya popped out of her chair and shook hands with both Cortez parents.

"I'm Maya Sinclair," she said. "It's great to meet you, Mr. and Mrs. Cortez."

"So, you're a Spy Kid from OSS-London," Dad said. "Funny, we didn't hear about you in our briefing this morning."

"Oh, it was a last-minute transfer," Maya said. "A Spy Kid exchange program they're trying out. I'm staying at OSS headquarters. And they sent Gerti Giggles to London HQ to take my place. It's just for the month."

"Well, welcome to America," Dad said. "We hope that you like it. Ingrid and I have been very happy here."

"Oh, Gregorio," Ingrid replied, touching Dad playfully on his big, square chin. "That was sweet."

Oh, no! Carmen thought. Mom and Dad are getting all mushy in front of Maya! How dorky is that?

"So, are you done with your hacking already?" Carmen broke in. "I thought you had a *lot* of work to do."

"Well, we never have so much work that we can't have dinner with our children," Mom said. Then she caught Carmen's desperate look.

"But we can see you're almost done, anyway," Mom added. "And you're right, Carmen, we *do* have to finish that high-clearance break-in before night falls on Nairobi. Gregorio?"

"Huh?" Dad said. Then he caught his wife's pointed look. With a shrug, he followed her out of the kitchen.

"Keep up the good work," Dad called over his shoulder to Carmen and Juni.

Carmen gave Maya an apologetic look as her parents disappeared from view.

"Well, those were the 'rents," she said. "They're great but, well, they can be a little—"

"Cool!" Maya said. "How did you get such with-it parents?"

Carmen had been about to say "nerdy." But then she looked at Juni. He returned her glance, and they both shrugged.

17

"Just lucky, I guess," Juni said. Then Juni couldn't help himself from taking a cookie from the jar and hurling it at his big sister. It hit her right in the back of the head.

Carmen spun around to glare at her brother. "You are such a . . . sturgleworm!"

"Hey, don't call me names," Juni said, grinning tauntingly at his sister. "It's not my fault your spy reflexes are slow."

"Little brothers," Carmen complained. She stalked back to the table and flopped into her chair next to Maya. Her new friend placed a sympathetic hand on her shoulder.

"I guess that's what happens when your partner is a ten-year-old boy," she said.

"Hey!" Juni said, twisting to face Maya with his fists on his hips. "That wasn't very nice."

"Well, neither was throwing the cookie at your sister," Maya said. "You *are* a worm."

Maya's words were hurtful. And Juni got a heavy, icky feeling in his gut. It was kind of a cold lump. He hadn't eaten any extrasweet Slushies that day, so he decided the cold feeling must mean something. Something bad.

Or maybe he was just mad.

Juni turned on his heel and stomped over to the

back door. He needed some time alone.

Just before he opened the door, though, something caught his eye. It was a large, cardboard box, stashed beneath the small table where Mom and Dad kept the mail.

But this was no ordinary mail.

It was a package from Uncle Machete. And that could mean only one thing—new gadgets!

Glancing over his shoulder, Juni saw that Carmen and Maya were totally ignoring him. They were deep into conversation about some movie star's hairdo.

This time, though, Juni was psyched that his sister and her new friend were dissing him. That meant he'd get first crack at Uncle Machete's latest inventions!

Juni slit open the box and began to rummage inside. He pulled out a tiny rubber box.

"Supercompacted field tent," the label said. "Sleeps four. Pool table not included."

"Nice . . ." Juni said. Next, he found a booklet that Uncle Machete had written.

"*Gadgetry and the Great Outdoors*," Juni read. "Homework! Huh. I'll save this for later."

Juni stuffed the booklet into his pocket and continued to rummage through the box. After happening upon a tube of Superspicy Firebeams, he pulled out two blue baseball caps. On the front of the caps were white OSS logos.

"We have lots of spy gear like this," Juni mused. "I wonder why Uncle Machete would send us more."

Then, Juni spotted a white tag sticking out of one hat's inner brim. He grabbed it and squinted at the fine print: "Purple = truth. Green = half-truth. Yellow = white lie. Red = big, fat lie."

"*In*-teresting," Juni whispered. He slipped the hat on and peered into the small mirror that hung next to the back door.

"My name is Juni Rocket Racer Rebelde Cortez," he said.

The white OSS logo turned purple! It glowed a bit before turning white again.

"Wow," Juni breathed. "It works! How about, 'I'm sorry for throwing a cookie at my sister?'"

Juni looked into the mirror excitedly and watched the cap's logo turn yellow.

"A white lie," Juni said with a tiny smile. "Got *that* right. Now, I'll go for a big, fat lie. Let's see . . . 'I am a seven-foot-tall basketball star.'"

Juni stared at his reflection, eagerly waiting for the OSS logo to turn red. But instead, it just went a little fuzzy. Then it turned a gray, sludgy color.

"Oh," Juni whispered in disappointment. "I

guess this is one of those gadgets that Uncle Machete hasn't perfected quite yet."

Juni took off the cap and turned to the girls. He tossed the cap onto the table and said, "Here, since you guys are so fashion crazy. Try this on for size."

Maya picked up the hat. Then she slipped it over her shiny, dark hair.

"Anyway, as I was saying, Carmen . . ." Maya said. As Maya chatted on, Juni glanced at the logo on her OSS cap.

Then he did a double take.

And then he almost gasped!

The OSS logo had changed color—to a glowing, garish shade of red.

And that meant one thing.

Maya was a big, fat liar!

Juni's spy instincts kicked in. He had to warn Carmen immediately. Which meant he had to get her away from Maya—somehow.

"Hey, Carmen," Juni said. "I guess you don't want me to show you the sweet new gadget Uncle Machete made for you."

"What gadget?" Carmen said, her eyebrows shooting up.

Ha! Juni had her now!

"It's in the pantry," Juni said. "Come with me—*alone*—and I'll show you."

"Excuse me, Maya," Carmen said, getting up from the table. Juni grabbed the spare OSS cap and hurried across the room. Carmen followed him into the pantry and crossed her arms over her chest.

"Where is it?" she demanded.

"There is no 'it,'" Juni whispered. "I just had to get you out of there. Something's wrong about Maya, *if* that is her real name."

"You're right," Carmen said, nodding at Juni.

"I am?" Juni said. He was surprised Carmen was seeing his point of view so quickly.

"Yes. That something is *you*, Juni," Carmen said. She pointed at her brother in annoyance. "You've been pestering us since we got home."

Juni slapped his forehead. Then he showed Carmen Uncle Machete's OSS cap.

"Listen," he said. "This cap detects lies, see?"

He showed Carmen the color code on the inside of the cap.

"The minute Maya put the cap on, the logo turned bright red!" Juni continued.

Carmen's face fell for a moment. Then her jaw hardened again.

"You know how faulty Uncle Machete's new inventions can be," she said. She grabbed the cap and planted it on top of Juni's damp curls. "Prove it."

"Okay," Juni said, adjusting the cap on his head. "Here's a truth. Your name is Carmen Elizabeth Juanita Echo Sky Brava Cortez."

Then Juni looked at his sister.

"Okay, what color is the logo?" he asked.

"Purple," she said.

"See, that's the color for truth!"

"Okay, so tell a big fat lie," Carmen challenged.

"It's the dead of winter outside," Juni said.

Carmen squinted at the cap.

"It's a gross, gray color now," she said with a smug nod. "Far from red. See, I told you!"

"What?!" Juni squeaked. He grabbed a can of tomatoes off the pantry shelf and gazed into his reflection in the shiny, silver top. Carmen was right! Then Juni realized something.

"Hey, I know why it didn't turn red," he said. "It *is* the dead of winter. Somewhere in the world, anyway."

"You're groping, Juni," Carmen said. "And I think I know why. You're jealous!"

"Jealous?" Juni retorted. He ripped the cap from his head in frustration. "Of *what*?"

"Maya!" Carmen said. "She's the best Spy Kid

you've ever seen and you know it. And . . . she thinks I'm cool."

"She's *pretending* to think you're cool," Juni said. "Carmen, I swear, the cap turned bright, bright red on Maya's head. There was no question about it. She's hiding something!"

"How about I put your little theory to the test?" Carmen said.

Before Juni could stop her, Carmen flounced back into the kitchen. She walked up to Maya, who was leaning against the kitchen counter, nibbling a cookie.

"I have an idea," Carmen said to the new spy. "Why don't you spend the night here tonight? We could watch a video. It'll be fun."

"Really?" Maya said. Her face lit up. "Oh, Carmen, that would be great. I mean, my quarters at the OSS are comfortable and all. But, I must admit, it's *much* more homey here."

"It's settled then," Carmen said. She glared at her brother defiantly. Then she grabbed a cordless phone and tossed it to Maya. "Why don't you just call the OSS and let them know. And I'll tell my Mom and Dad."

And *I'll* start rigging up surveillance equipment, Juni thought darkly. We've got a possible double agent under our roof. It's going to be a long night!

CHAPTER 3

An hour later, Carmen and Maya were hanging out in the family room. They were wearing pajamas and eating ice cream. Juni was skulking just outside the room, eavesdropping. But so far, Maya hadn't said anything suspicious.

In fact, in Juni's opinion, his sister and the double agent were talking about the most boring thing imaginable—makeup.

"I've *got* to ask you, Maya," Carmen was saying, "I noticed your lipstick stayed on through the whole sturgleworm incident this morning. How *do* you do it?"

"Oh, it's this brilliant stuff I got from the OSS lab," Maya said. "You can have some if you like."

The OSS is manufacturing *makeup*?! Juni thought. What's happening to my world? He peeked around the family room door. Maya was rifling through a turquoise makeup case.

"You see," Maya continued, extracting a pink

tube from the case. "This looks like an ordinary lip gloss in the shade of 'Cotton Candy.'"

Maya smeared some of the pink stuff onto her lips.

"But this lipstick has a double identity," she added with a grin. She turned the tube upside down and pressed a tiny button. Immediately, a whirring propeller erupted from the lip gloss. It was powerful enough to lift Maya clear off the couch. She flew across the room! Then she turned the propeller off and landed lightly on her feet.

"Oh, man, I've *gotta* get one of those," Juni exclaimed. Then he clapped his hand over his mouth.

"Juni!" Carmen cried. She leaped off the couch and bounded over to the door to grab her brother. She started to shake him by the shoulders, but she was laughing too hard to do any damage.

"I should be mad at you for spying on us," she said. "On the other hand, I just got to hear my *brother* wish for pink lipstick!"

"Carmen . . ." Juni warned.

"I'll tell Dad to put it on your Christmas list," Carmen giggled.

"You better not!" Juni yelled.

"Or maybe you would prefer the purple

eye shadow/invisi-dust," Maya said as she popped the lip gloss back into her case. "It explodes, covering the wearer with shimmering dust, which makes her invisible for forty-five minutes. Plus, it's really pretty! It would look great with your red hair, Juni!"

"Shut! Up!" Juni bellowed at the top of his lungs.

"Juni!"

Juni froze and slowly turned around. Naturally, it was his parents. They were both wearing white karate togs, and they had their arms crossed over their chests. They'd snuck up behind him—again! How did they always *do* that?

"That is no way to talk to our guest *or* your older sister," Mom said.

"Even if you *were* provoked," Dad said, giving Carmen a hard look. She swallowed her last giggle and tried to look serious.

"Juni started it," she said. "He was eavesdropping on us!"

"Let's keep the tattling to a minimum, shall we?" Mom said. "It's almost your bedtime and I'd appreciate, oh, ten minutes of non chaos."

"Okay," Juni and Carmen said sheepishly.

"Now, your father and I will be in the basement

training room," Mom said. She walked over to Juni to give him a kiss good night. "You know, I'm just one test away from my quadruple black belt. Your dad's going to help me train."

"Cooool," Maya breathed.

"Don't stay up too late," Dad said, stepping over to kiss Carmen on the top of the head. Then he looked at the new Spy Kid. "Maya, you'll sleep in the extra bed in Carmen's room. Just let us know if you need anything."

"Thanks, Mr. and Mrs. Cortez," Maya said quietly.

"No problem, honey," Mom said. She slung an arm around Maya's shoulders and gave her a little squeeze. "Sweet dreams."

With that, the Cortez parents went downstairs to punch and kick the night away. And Maya sank onto the couch, looking despondent.

"Is something wrong?" Carmen asked gently. She sat down next to Maya on the couch. Juni flopped into Dad's easy chair and glowered at the two of them.

"No," Maya said shakily. "In fact, I'd say your parents are nothing but right."

Carmen shot Juni a quick glance. Their eyes met. For once, silent agreement passed between them. They knew they'd really lucked out in the parental department. Even if Mom and Dad could be a *little* dorky. Carmen turned back to Maya.

"You know . . ." she said to her hesitantly, "you haven't mentioned your family."

"Oh, you mean the OSS?" Maya scoffed.

"What?" Carmen asked. "Don't you have parents? Or siblings? Even . . . an aunt or cousin?"

"I did once," Maya said quietly—"have parents, that is. But . . . I don't anymore."

Carmen flashed Juni another look. Then she put a hand on Maya's shoulder.

"Do you want to talk about it?" she asked.

Maya shrugged.

"Just your classic story—orphan girl gets adopted by the OSS to save the world," Maya joked. "That's all."

Both Carmen and Juni knew that *wasn't* all. But clearly, Maya didn't want to share the rest of her painful story. The sadness in her eyes said enough. She was alone, without any family. Even Juni could see that was the truth.

"Wow . . ." Carmen said softly.

But before she could say anything else, a siren sounded.

The flat-screen TV began flashing two words: YELLOW ALERT!

Mom and Dad came bounding up the basement stairs. And Juni slapped his hands together and jumped off his chair.

"That's the OSS," he said.

"You know how it is," Carmen said to Maya. "We'll be right back."

"Looks like it's mission time!" Juni announced.

CHAPTER 4

Thirty seconds after the alarm sounded, the four Cortezes were clustered around their information hub in Mom and Dad's bedroom. Mom pressed a few eye shadows and lipsticks on her vanity table. Her mirror transformed into a video screen, and the tray of cosmetics flipped over to become a computer keyboard. Mom typed in that day's top-secret password. The chiseled face of their head honcho—Devlin—appeared on the screen.

"That was quick! Hello, Cortezes," Devlin said. "I won't keep you because I know it's bedtime. And believe me, you four are going to need your rest for this mission. It's going to take you to Mortille."

"Never heard of it," Dad said. He was standing behind his wife. Carmen and Juni were at his side.

"Hardly anyone has," Devlin replied grimly. "It's an obscure island somewhere in the Pacific. A psychopathic recluse has been in control of the island for the past fifteen years. Once upon a time this villain was a mild-mannered ear, nose, and throat doctor named Leonard Snortle. But something went very wrong with Dr. Snortle. One sneeze too many? Frustration over the common cold? We'll never know. Our intel on Dr. Snortle is embarrassingly small. All we do know is he is now pure evil, and he goes by the name of Sinus.

"Sinus has wired Mortille from beach to volcano," Devlin continued. "Now, he's ready to make his move."

"What kind of move?" Juni said, clenching his jaw.

"A computer virus," Devlin replied. "Sinus has built a device on Mortille called the SNZ 100. We're not sure exactly what it is, but we do know it's equipped to transmit a powerful virus to every satellite in the earth's orbit."

"That's 3,042 satellites belonging to fifty-nine countries," Carmen said automatically. When the rest of her family turned to gape at her, she shrugged. "What? I'm a hacker. It's my job to know these things."

Then Carmen turned back to Devlin.

"Why is Sinus doing this?" she asked.

"I wish I knew, Carmen," Devlin said, his forehead

furrowing in anger. "All we know for sure is—he wants to take over the world.

"Cortezes—we've installed a hyperspeed drill sub at checkpoint Number Thirty-six for you. It's programmed to take you to Mortille. It's also equipped with a computerized intelligence system that will familiarize you with the island."

With that, Devlin's transmission ended. Juni turned to his family.

"*Another* guy who wants to take over the planet?" he complained. "What is it with all these super-villains?"

"Oh, come on," Mom said, ruffling Juni's curls. "You know you love saving the world as much as we do. Now I want you to hop right into bed. We all need a good night's rest. I'll be back in a minute to tuck you in."

"Mom!" Juni complained. "I'm an OSS spy! I don't need to be tucked in!"

"Oh," Mom said, shooting Dad a sorrowful look. "I guess you're right. And I guess you won't be needing the milk and cookies I was going to bring you, either."

"Um, tucking in," Juni sputtered quickly. "Yeah, I don't see a problem with that. See you in five minutes, Mom. But let's keep it classified, okay?"

"Okay," she promised with a grin. Juni scrambled out the door. Then Mom turned to her daughter.

"Carmen?" she asked. "Milk and cookies before the big mission?"

"I'm okay, Mom," Carmen replied. "But you might want to give Maya some TLC. She's an orphan, you know."

"We *didn't* know that," Mom said somberly. "What a tragedy. Like your father and I always say, Family is worth more than anything. More than money, more than power."

"I know. It's mega-sad," Carmen said, slumping against the bedroom wall. "And on top of that, Juni doesn't trust Maya! He thinks she's hiding something. But clearly, he's just jealous. Y'know, because we're friends and all."

"Don't worry about that," Dad said. "Your mother and I will talk to Juni after this mission is completed. But now, let's get to bed. We'll pack up our gear for the assignment in the morning."

By 6 A.M. the next day, the spies were in the kitchen. They were simultaneously eating breakfast and strapping themselves into their gizmo-laden spy vests and utility belts. Meanwhile, Dad walked over to a keypad mounted on the wall next to the garage door. He typed in some coordinates.

"Maya?" he called out as he typed.

"Yes, Mr. Cortez?" Maya said. She was sitting at the table, eating a breakfast of granola and fruit.

"I'm programming our self-propelled electric car. It will take you back to the OSS's HQ while we head out on our mission," Dad told her. "But, please, come back and visit us any time."

"Whatever," Juni muttered under his breath. Irritably, he planted an OSS cap onto his head.

"No problem," Maya said. She stood up and gave Juni a cool look. She put her cereal bowl in the sink and turned to his father. "I really appreciate the ride, Mr. Cortez."

Then Maya looked at Carmen, who was filling her canteen with her favorite flavor of Fooglie Fruit Punch—Kumquat-Kiwi.

"And *you* better call me the minute you get back," Maya said to her. "Maybe we can go to the cinema or the mall."

"What are friends for?" Carmen replied. As Maya headed to the garage, Carmen felt a wave of happiness wash over her. Maya was *so* cool. Carmen could already envision years of best-friendship with her. They'd go shopping and go on double dates and maybe even do more missions together. . . .

Suddenly, Carmen jolted herself out of her dream.

This is no time to be daydreaming about going to the mall, she admonished herself. It's mission time.

Carmen walked to the garage door and peeked out the window. Maya was climbing into the Cortezes' electric car. She paused to give Carmen a little wave. And then she was gone.

Carmen sighed and turned around. As usual, her mom seemed to know exactly what she was thinking.

"How about we invite Maya for a shopping trip as soon as we get back?" she whispered to Carmen.

"How about we get going?" Juni proposed instead. "Our drill sub is waiting."

Within a few minutes, the family was standing on a wooden dock inside Checkpoint #36, otherwise known as the OSS's oceanside boathouse. They were gaping at their new vehicle—the drill sub.

"It's the coolest!" Juni breathed.

"It's beautiful!" Dad agreed.

Outfitted with the latest in computer-driven periscopes and control panels, the drill sub was sleek and swoosh shaped. It had a purple and turquoise paint job and portholes for every member of the family. On its nose was a gigantic titanium drill. It was perfect for those missions where washing up on the beach would blow your cover in a big way. Instead, the drill sub was built to bore through sand, rock, even petrified lava. And the Cortezes planned to drive it straight to the middle of Mortille, where they hoped they would elude Sinus's surveillance.

One by one, the spies filed into the sub.

Dad sat at the steering wheel.

Mom cross-checked the weapons systems.

Carmen booted up the computer.

And Juni made sure the minifridge was stocked with plenty of food.

Then they locked the hatch and exchanged determined looks.

"Fasten your seat belts, children," Dad said. "We're going under."

Burble-burble-burble-burble.

Slowly, the drill sub sank into the water. Carmen and Juni watched the walls of the boathouse drift away. Soon, they were under the sea. The water became darker and murkier as the sub sank deeper.

"Ready for hyperspeed?" Dad asked.

"Ready!" replied four voices.

Um . . . *four* voices?

Carmen, Juni, Mom, and Dad twisted in their seats and peered into the back of the sub. Strapped into the extra seat, wearing her Spy Kid gear, was a surprise stowaway.

Juni's fists trembled with rage. Mom and Dad's eyes widened in shock. And Carmen's face broke into a big grin.

"Maya!" she exclaimed.

CHAPTER 5

"**H**ullo," Maya said to the stunned Cortez family. She was smiling sweetly. "I thought you might want a spot of help."

Juni unhooked his seat belt and leaped to his feet. He stalked to the back of the drill sub.

"If we had needed your help," he fumed, "Devlin might have assigned you to this case. Or my Dad wouldn't have sent you back to HQ. *Or we would have asked for help!*"

"Juni!" Carmen cried.

But Juni ignored his sister. He continued to glare down at Maya. He expected Maya to shoot back some snide retort. But instead, her face crumpled. Actual tears formed in the corners of her big, brown eyes. Then she gazed wanly at Mom and Dad.

"I . . . I know I did the wrong thing hitching along like this," she said softly. "But my missions for the OSS are always solo. And . . . it's lonely! You just looked like you were having so much fun together. And I really did want to help you, because you made me feel so welcome."

"Maya," Dad said sternly. "You're right—this was the wrong thing to do. The Cortezes work as a team—a very tight team. We can't just spontaneously become the Cortezes plus one Sinclair. It would be . . . awkward."

Dad gave Mom an uncomfortable glance. Then they both looked at Maya's trembling lower lip.

Oh, Maya's good, Juni thought. She's pushing all of Mom and Dad's buttons. But surely they'll see through her little crybaby act.

"The thing is, honey," Mom said quietly to Dad, "we don't really have time to take her back to HQ. And she *does* look so sad."

What?! Juni thought in outrage.

"I guess there'd be no harm in letting her tag along," Dad muttered back to Mom.

What, *what*?! Juni thought in further outrage. He couldn't believe this. Maya Sinclair had duped his entire family. And now she was going to wreck their entire mission—Juni just knew it.

He stomped back to his seat and glared at his parents.

"So, Maya stays?" he demanded.

"Maya stays," Mom said, shooting Dad another glance.

"Maya stays," Carmen said, throwing her friend a triumphant smile.

"I guess I'll stay, then," Maya said. She quickly flicked the tears away from her eyes and grinned at the Cortezes. Then she buckled her seat belt and nodded at Dad.

"As we were saying, sir," she announced, "ready for hyperspeed."

"Sir?" Dad said, raising his eyebrows. Then he turned back around in his seat. "She called me, 'sir.' Heh-heh-heh."

Juni rolled his eyes. But he couldn't hold a grudge. He had to focus on the mission. His dad was pulling back on the hyperspeed throttle. Which meant that, in approximately 3.6 seconds, the drill sub would be traveling through the ocean at a speed so speedy that blinking, talking, even *eating* would be impossible. And for Juni, that was pretty speedy.

Fwoooooooom!

And they were off! As the hyperspeed kicked in, the drill sub's passengers were pressed flat against their seat backs. Their lips flapped around their cheeks, and their eyes were pinned open.

"How . . . soon . . . till . . . we get . . . there . . . ?" Carmen asked with difficulty.

"Only . . . twenty . . . minutes," Dad grunted in reply. He was staring out of his porthole as the drill sub's autopilot darted around stalagmites, boulders, and shipwrecks on the ocean floor.

"That is . . . " Dad added, "if everything . . . goes . . . as . . . planned."

Of course, that's when the plan went seriously awry. Or, to be more specific, that's when an army of sharks suddenly swarmed around the drill sub, knocking the vehicle off course.

Not to mention, upside down.

"Aaaaaahhh!" the Spy Kids screamed as Dad struggled to right the drill sub. He threw the hyperspeed throttle into reverse. The drill sub chugged down to a crawl.

And the sharks fell upon the drill sub, wriggling like mad.

"Just a school of sharks. No biggie," Juni said nervously. His eyes darted from porthole to porthole. All he could see was a crush of slithery, silvery shark bodies. "Good thing the drill sub isn't a fish," he said. "Otherwise, we'd be in the middle of a feeding frenzy right now!"

"Right, son," Dad said, flipping a few buttons.

"That is a very good thing indeed. It is also a good thing that our vehicle here is equipped with Zap-O-Skin. Now the activator button is . . ."

"Right here, Dad," Carmen said, pointing to a lightning bolt–shaped button on the sub's control panel.

"Ah, yes," Dad said. Then he glared through the portholes. "Get ready to dance, fishies!"

Just before Dad mashed the button with his finger, a voice piped up from the back of the drill sub: "Ahem. Mr. Cortez . . . sir?"

Dad's finger paused above the Zap-O-Skin button. He glanced over his shoulder.

"Yes, Maya?"

"Well, um, sir, are you sure it's such a good idea to shock the sharks?" Maya asked. "It might only anger them further."

"Oh, and I suppose you'd rather sit here while they gnaw on our drill sub?" Juni said. "Or maybe you'd like to turn around altogether, is that it?"

"No," Maya said. "I was just wonder—"

"We're spies," Juni retorted. "We don't have time to wonder!"

With that, Juni reached out and hit the Zap-O-Skin activator.

ZOOOOTTTZZZZ!

Immediately, the drill sub's entire exterior was

electrified. And the sharks got the shock of their lives. As bright green sparks zapped through the water, they leaped away from the sub.

The twitching sharks backed away from the sub and hovered in a cluster between the drill sub and the mouth of an underwater cave.

Juni pressed his face to a porthole and gazed at the school of wriggling sharks.

"Whoa!" he said. "There must be three hundred sharks out there. And . . . wait, what's up with their noses?"

"What are you talking about?" Carmen said, peeking over Juni's shoulder. When she got a good look at the sharks, she yelped in surprise.

"Mom, Dad," she said. "You've got to see this."

The whole Cortez crew gazed out the porthole at the strangest sharks they'd ever seen. Their bodies were those of ordinary sharks—slick, silver skin; vacant black eyes; and razor-sharp gills. But instead of having streamlined, pointy heads, the sharks had *human* noses. And they were the hugest schnozzes the Cortezes had ever seen.

"I can practically count their nose hairs!" Carmen said.

"Their nostrils are as big as dinner plates!" Mom said.

"And look at how they're flaring," Juni said in fascination. "It's almost like they're sniffing us! Clearly, these mutant sharks are the work of Sinus!"

"Precisely why we can't sit around staring at them," Dad said. "This is no aquarium. Crew— strap yourselves in. Resume hyperspeed!"

As the family snapped their seat belts shut, Dad flicked a series of switches and pulled back on the hyperspeed throttle. And . . . nothing happened.

"Gregorio?" Mom said nervously.

"I . . . I don't know what the problem is," Dad said, flicking a few backup buttons. "The drill sub is in hyperspeed. We should be moving at a thousand knots per hour."

Juni peered out the porthole at the crowd of sharks.

"Um . . . Dad?" he said in a quavering voice.

"What is it, Juni," Dad said absently. He was still working the control panel like mad.

"I think I just realized why the sharks have those big nostrils!" Juni said. "Look!"

The crew gazed out at the sharks again. The fishes' nostrils had flared to the size of beach balls. And they were fluttering wildly.

The sharks were sniffing with all their might.

And their noses were so powerful, the drill sub was immobilized.

Scratch that. The drill sub *was* moving—but it was moving backward! The Big-Nose Sharks were sucking the sub toward the underwater cave.

"Uh, Dad," Carmen said, typing on the drill sub's computer. "I hate to be the bearer of more bad news, but that cave? I've just located it on our underwater mapping system. It's a black hole-in-the-ground."

"You don't mean . . ." Juni gasped.

"Yup," Carmen said, nodding grimly. "A black hole-in-the-ground is a vicious vortex. Whatever gets sucked in gets smashed flat. And never emerges."

"Ay, this is *not* good," Dad said. "But don't you worry, children. Your mother and I will get you out of this. Ingrid, how *will* we get out of this?"

"All we need is a thermonuclear velocitizer," Mom said, nodding confidently.

"That would be perfect," Carmen agreed. "But, uh, we don't have one."

"Oh!" Mom said, her shoulders sagging. She looked at her husband in panic.

"There's got to be another way out of this." Dad bellowed. "Carmen? Is there any other information on the system? Some background on Sinus's mutants?"

Carmen typed rapidly, searching the system desperately for more information.

"All it says about Sinus's weaponry is, 'The nose knows!'" Carmen said with exasperation. "Honestly, of all the times for a riddle!"

"Um, ahem . . ." piped up that all-too-familiar voice from the back of the drill sub. Juni rolled his eyes. Now what? He looked back at Maya. She seemed to be deep in thought.

She was biting her lip nervously.

Then, suddenly, she turned to Carmen.

"I think the riddle may mean," Maya proposed, "that these creatures' strength lies in their noses. But maybe that's their weakness as well."

"What . . . ?" Juni said, rolling his eyes.

"What if we gave them something really rotten to smell?" Maya suggested, with a glint in her eye.

The entire Cortez family paused for a moment and gazed admiringly at Maya.

"Maya," Dad said, nodding appreciatively. "That idea is so brilliant, I should have thought of it myself."

Juni was . . . doubtful.

There had to be a catch.

"Okay, Maya," Juni challenged. "But how do you expect us to come up with a stink bad enough to conquer these big-nosed nudnicks?"

Maya frowned.

And then she grinned.

And *then* she hopped out of her seat and rushed to the drill sub's minifridge.

"I saw you stash a meatball-and-chocolate-chip hero in here, Juni," she said. She pulled a large, foil-wrapped sandwich out of the fridge.

"I propose," she continued, "we add a little carbolic acid to this baby. Then we pop it into the microwave. After that, we should have a pretty stinky mess on our hands."

Juni felt his blood run cold.

"My . . . *hero?*" He squeaked. He'd *known* there'd be a catch.

"That's a perfect idea, Maya," Mom exclaimed. "Let's get busy. Crew—get out your nose clips."

They all extracted lime-green clips from their utility belts and squeezed them onto their noses. Then Maya began doctoring Juni's lunch. By the time she'd finished with it, it was a steaming, burnt husk. Juni could practically *see* how bad it smelled. He heaved a deep sigh.

"All wight, Baya," Dad said through his plugged nostrils. "Led's see if dis worzs."

He gingerly took the molten sandwich from Maya and put it into the drill sub's ejection shoot.

Then he shot it at the deep-sniffing Big-Nose Sharks.

At first, the mutant creatures took no notice of the stinky sandwich. They just continued to sniff away, drawing the drill sub even closer to the lethal hole-in-the-ground.

But then, their fluttering nostrils began to flare in disgust.

Their black eyes began to redden.

Their rows of sharp teeth gritted in pain.

And finally, the creatures could stand the putrid sandwich no longer. Screeching in horror, they spun around and slithered far into the murky water.

A few seconds later, they disappeared altogether.

"We did it!" Juni yelled. His yell careened out of control as the drill sub broke out of the sharks' powerful sniffs and leaped back into hyperspeed.

"Great job, everyone," Dad said, taking off his nose clip as the drill sub hurtled through the sea. "But there's no time to celebrate. We've still got to make it to Mortille. Sinus could be enacting his evil plan even as we speak!"

CHAPTER 6

Only a few minutes later, the family and Maya were staring at the island of Mortille. The *bottom* of the island of Mortille, that is. And a tropical paradise it definitely wasn't. The sand was strewn with bright purple, red, and pink metal spikes, molded to look like coral. Giant mechanical jellyfish trailing electronic stingers floated around the coral. So, too, did robotic sharks with four-inch teeth.

"Nice of Sinus to put out the welcome mat," Carmen said dryly.

"That's okay," Dad replied. He pushed a few buttons on the control panel. "Our drill sub has a thick skin."

And with a growling, grinding noise, the titanium screw on the sub's nose began spinning.

"Hang on to your seats, kids," Mom cried.

With that, Dad plowed straight into the ocean floor.

Bzzzzzwhhyyyrrrrrrrr!

The drill sub cut easily through the sandy ocean bed. Then it sliced through gushy mud. And finally, it bored through a layer of rock. They'd reached the center of Mortille.

Then the drill sub veered upward. With a few more whirls of its giant, titanium screw, the sub burst out of the ground. And finally, the vehicle came to a rest. The crew blinked as shafts of bright sunlight poured through the portholes. They'd landed in a glade of palm trees deep in the jungle.

"Wow," Juni breathed, gazing through the windows. He saw coconut palms and banana trees, plants with leaves the size of elephants' ears, chittering monkeys and chattering toucans. It was like a tropical vacation spot!

"Okay, we've made it," Mom said, jolting Juni out of his reverie. "Now, let's make a plan of action. Carmen, can you brief us on the island?"

"No prob," Carmen said, turning to the computer's keyboard and typing briskly. On the screen appeared an overhead view of Mortille. The island was shaped like a triangle with two round coves cut into its wide bottom.

"It sorta looks like a . . . nose!" Juni said.

Then the computer zoomed in for a closer look.

An X ray showed electrical circuits inside almost every tree and rock!

"The island of Mortille," Carmen began, "is completely wired. Sinus has electrified one third of the trees, rocks, and shrubs. Anyone who touches them will get a shock."

"Real back to nature of him," Juni said with a sneer.

"Well, Sinus *does* like to play God," Carmen said. "He controls everything that happens on Mortille from his headquarters. It's a sterile fortress called the Ol-Factory. He lives and works there guarded by dozens of security brutes. In fact, he never seems to leave."

"Probably too afraid of getting shocked by his own evil devices," Mom said. "What else, Carmen?"

"We also have to watch out for the so-called Quick Goo," Carmen said. An image of a bubbling patch of sand came onto the computer screen. "It's sort of like quicksand, but much more disgusting. It'll swallow you up completely in twenty-five seconds."

"Anything else?" Mom asked Carmen.

"Let's see . . ." Carmen said, typing away at the computer. "Watch out for enhanced poison ivy—

it'll give you torturous bumps. And Sinus has planted gas-passers around the island that shoot supersmelly vapors at you. Oh, and here's something else," Carmen said, peering at the screen. "It looks like there are surveillance cameras, microphones, and speakers all over the island. Security is *really* tight."

WHOOO-WHOOO-WHOOO-WHOOO!

"There's an alarm." Dad yelled over the noise.

"*An* alarm?" Juni shouted. He clapped his hands over his ears. "There must be thousands of speakers on this island! That Sinus is paranoid!"

"As soon as we activate the drill sub's cloaking device, we'll disappear from his radar," Mom yelled. She flipped some switches on the control panel. "But first, we have to make a plan. Kids— you do reconnaissance while Dad and I man the computer here at the drill sub. Send any information you find on SNZ 100 back to us here. We'll analyze the data and join you when we've figured out how to foil the villain's plan."

"It'll be a cinch!" Dad said with a nod.

"Don't you worry, Mr. and Mrs. Cortez," Maya said brightly. "I'm sure we'll have no problem finding that nasty contraption."

After some quick good-bye kisses from Mom,

the three kids popped the drill sub's hatch and tumbled out into jungle.

Carmen leaped to the mossy ground first. A huge palm leaf brushed her leg and made a crackling noise. Then, it jolted Carmen with a bright pink spark.

"Ouch!" she cried, slapping her leg with her hand. "That felt like a bee sting."

Juni jumped out next. He steadied himself on a palm tree trunk as he landed.

SSSzzzzzz, the tree crackled.

And then it shocked Juni with a loud *Ziiitttz*!

"Ack!" Juni cried. He yanked his hand away from the tree. "I got shocked, too."

Maya perched for a moment in the drill sub's doorway. She seemed to be looking at a precise spot on the ground. Then she jumped. Juni waited to hear another zapping noise, but Maya remained unshocked.

She turned to Carmen and Juni and shrugged.

"Lucky me," she said with a grin.

"Naturally," Juni grumbled.

Mom and Dad waved good-bye to the kids and closed the sub's hatch. An instant later, the entire craft began to blur. And shimmer. And finally, it disappeared altogether. Immediately, the island's blaring security alarm halted. Juni giggled.

"Now you see it," he said, "now you don't."

"Cool!" Maya breathed.

Carmen pushed a button on her spy watch.

"Mom, Dad?" she said.

"Copy," said Dad's voice from Carmen's watch. "Are we invisible?"

"Totally," Carmen replied. "The sub has completely disappeared."

"Perfect," Dad said. "Now, Carmen, I want you to go to the Ol-Factory. Coordinates are sixty-seven degrees west and thirty-eight degrees south."

"Right," Carmen said, typing the numbers into her spy watch.

"Plant bugs everywhere you can," Dad instructed. "That way, we'll hear about Sinus's plan. And Juni? You and Maya search for the SNZ 100. If you find it, send us the location."

"Me and *Maya*?" Juni complained.

"Juni . . . ." Now it was Mom's voice echoing out of Carmen's spy watch. And she had that soft, disappointed tone that made Juni cringe.

"All right," Juni grumbled. "Me and Maya. For the sake of the mission."

"Yes," Maya said, with a hard look in her eyes. "For the mission."

"Off you go then," Dad said through the spy watch. "Keep in touch. And good luck! Over and out."

With that, the kids began to trek through the jungle.

Carmen led the way, heading southwest in the direction of the Ol-Factory. She pulled an automatic weed whacker from her utility belt. Its hinged, motorized blade swung back and forth and up and down, hacking thick, jungly plants out of Carmen's way. Juni followed in his sister's path.

"Mom and Dad should have sent *me* to do the bugging," Juni complained to the back of Carmen's head. "Then you and Maya could work together and talk about girlie stuff."

"Focus on the mission, Juni," Carmen said over her shoulder. "And face it! You're a klutz. You wouldn't have been in the Ol-Factory for more than a minute before you tripped over something and got caught."

"Would not!" Juni yelled—just as his toe hit a patch of bright orange mushrooms in the trail.

PSSSSSSSSSS!

"What's that!" Juni cried, jumping backward. A burst of bright yellow vapor was hissing out of the mushroom patch.

"It's a gas-passer!" Carmen cried. "Your nose clips."

Carmen whipped her clip out of her vest and squeezed it over her nostrils. But it was too late for Juni.

His nose was already filled with the most rancid reek he'd ever run across.

It was like skunk squared. Or mold multiplied.

"Urrrgh," Juni groaned. His eyes crossed and he fell over.

"See?" Carmen said nasally, nodding.

"Like you're so perfect," Juni grumbled. With shaking hands, he put on his nose clips and struggled to his feet.

Then he looked around, peering into the thick, green jungle foliage.

"Hey, where's Baya?" he said through his plugged nose. "Just like her to biss getting gassed."

Carmen glanced around, too.

"I don't know," she said worriedly. "I thought she was right behind you!"

"Well, it's not *my* fault if she can't keep up," Juni retorted.

"Keep up with what?" said a British voice. A few seconds later, Maya herself emerged from the brush and joined them. "Oooh, what stinks?"

"Where were you?" Juni said with a glower.

"I had to make a stop," Maya said. Her eyes darted back and forth nervously.

She's got shifty eyes, Juni thought. That's a sure sign of lying! It says so in every spy manual.

"What *sort* of stop?" Juni demanded.

"A stop that required a tree," Maya said with a glare. "And a bit of privacy. It's not like they have bathrooms in the middle of the jungle, you know!"

"Oh!" Juni blurted. He felt his cheeks go hot and knew he was turning bright red. "Well, never mind then."

"Nice comeback, Juni," Carmen giggled. She took off her nose clips and took a cautious sniff. The gas cloud seemed to have dissipated.

"Now if you two can try to avoid tearing each other limb from limb," she said, "I'm going to head to the Ol-Factory."

"No problem," Juni said coolly, swiping off his own nose clips. He stood on tiptoe and looked around. Then he pointed over Maya's shoulder. "We'll start our search for the SNZ 100 over there, on top of that hill. That way, we'll see more."

"Oh, I don't think so," Maya said quickly. She

pointed over *Juni's* shoulder. "See that faint mist over there? That means there must be a waterfall nearby. And *everyone* knows water is a powerful conductor for computer viruses. The SNZ 100 is sure to be over there."

"Oh, yeah?" Juni said.

"Yeah!" Maya said, glaring down at Juni.

"You know what?" Carmen shouted. "I'll make this easy for you."

She reached into the mulch beneath their feet and pulled out a long green vine. At least, it *looked* like a vine.

"Why don't you just follow this electrical cord, cleverly disguised as local plant life," she said rolling her eyes. "Honestly, guys! Remember Spy Tactics 101? Follow the trail!"

Maya turned pink and looked down.

"You're right, of course!" she said. Then she gave Carmen a hopeful look. "Thanks for the tip."

Carmen smiled at her new friend.

"No problem," she said. "That's what fellow spies do. They help each other out. Right, Juni?"

She glared hard at her brother.

"You're right," Juni said, kicking at a pile of dead leaves.

Sssssszzzzz-ZOTZ!

"Ow!" Juni squealed. He shook his freshly shocked foot.

Carmen stifled a giggle. Then she turned and began slicing her way through the jungle again. She knew Maya could handle Juni. Now s*he* had to handle finding the Ol-Factory.

CHAPTER 7

Carmen paused on the jungle trail and squinted up at the sun. Then she checked her coordinates with her spy watch.

"If my calculations are correct," she muttered, "I should reach the Ol-Factory in a quarter mile."

With renewed determination, she held out her auto-whack and turned its speed to "superhigh." It began hacking through thick leaves and palm shoots as fast as Carmen could follow. In fact she was practically running, until . . .

Thwack!

"Aaah!" Carmen cried. She'd collided with something hard. And tall. And flat.

"What the—?" Carmen said, gazing upward. At first, all she saw were more coconut palms, fluttering elephant ears, and chattering birds. But then she realized she was looking at the Ol-Factory— painted with the most brilliant camouflage she'd ever seen. It was a jungle scene so detailed, it was practically invisible.

"Well, two can play at that game!" Carmen said. She reached into one of her vest pockets and pulled out a piece of candy. Inspecting the label, she read: "Chameleo-Candy. Guaranteed to make you blend into any surroundings. Flavor—tangerine. Created by Machete Cortez."

Carmen popped the candy into her mouth and started chewing. Then she felt her face crinkle up with pure disgust.

"Tangerine?" she gulped. "More like . . . tomatoes. Rotten ones! Ew! Uncle Machete really needs to work on his recipe."

Finally, Carmen choked the candy down. Then she held her hand up. Instantly, it seemed to transform into a palm leaf dotted with squirming jungle bugs. She was practically invisible herself.

"Well, at least the Chameleo-Candy works," Carmen muttered.

She began feeling her way along the wall of the building. It went on and on, but Carmen could feel no windows or doors.

"This place is huge," Carmen breathed. "I've gotta figure out a way to get inside."

No sooner had the words left her mouth than

her invisible fingers closed around a corner of the invisible building. And that's when something happened.

A voice, clearly an electronic one, spoke to Carmen.

"Password?" the voice requested.

Carmen gulped. There'd been nothing on the drill sub's computer about a password! She'd have to wing it. She thought about everything she'd learned about Sinus. Her mind flitted from the Big Nose Sharks to the triangular shape of the island to the gas-passers.

And then . . . Carmen knew. The password had to be the thing that tied everything together in the sick world of Sinus.

"The password is—nose!" Carmen declared.

"Access denied," responded the flat, robotic voice.

"What?" Carmen cried. "But . . . okay, how about, um, snout?"

"Access denied."

"Schnozz?" Carmen cried desperately. "Sniffer? Schnozzle? Proboscis?"

"Access denied," the voice repeated.

"Who knows?" Carmen whispered, her shoulders slumping in defeat. But as the words left her mouth, something clicked in her head. That riddle—the one that had stumped her in the drill sub. Perhaps it wasn't a riddle at all, but a solution!

"The nose knows!" Carmen said triumphantly.

"Access . . ." the robotic voice said, "granted!"

"Whoo-hoo!" Carmen cried. Then she stumbled backward as the camouflaged corner cracked open before her. She slipped into the building, and the seamless doorway immediately closed behind her.

Carmen turned around and found herself in a corridor that sloped upward. The walls were as smooth and white as the outside of the building had been vibrant. Carmen felt like she'd stumbled into a futuristic spaceship. She looked down at herself and saw that she, too, had turned white and one-dimensional. She was blending into the scenery perfectly.

Carmen lifted her spy watch to her mouth and whispered, "Mom, Dad? I've made it to the Ol-Factory. I'm in!"

Then she waited for her Dad to respond. She expected him to say, "I'm proud of you, Carmenita!" in his silky, Spanish accent. Or even just, "Copy that."

But all Carmen heard was the rustle of static.

There was no answer.

All contact with her parents and the drill sub had been cut off!

Carmen lowered her spy watch and took a deep breath.

Okay, she thought. What could have happened?

She imagined her parents trapped in a puddle of supersucking Quick Goo. Or being zapped repeatedly by a shocking palm tree. Maybe they were coughing their way through a cloud of super-smelly gas!

Then Carmen shook her head.

"Mom and Dad are international superspies," she told herself quietly. "They've *got* to be all right. What's more, they've entrusted me with this job. I *have* to plant these bugs."

Carmen patted the side pocket in her cargo pants where she'd stashed dozens of tiny bugging devices. Each one was the size of a pencil dot, yet contained a complete audio recording system and teensy-tiny video camera. If Carmen planted the bugs all over the Ol-Factory, they would be able to gather all the information the Cortezes needed to take Sinus down.

Carmen tiptoed up the long, bright-white corridor. Then it forked off in two directions. One sloped upward, and the other went down.

"I'm guessing a power-hungry madman like Sinus would prefer a room with a view," Carmen mused. She chose the upward slanting corridor. She fished a tiny bug out of her pocket, licked its back, and stuck it to the wall.

She crept onward, planting more bugs as she went. The corridor began to twist.

And turn.

It even did a loop-de-loop.

Finally, Carmen huffed in exasperation.

"I feel like a mouse in a maze!" she whispered. "I'm a total reconnaissance reject!"

Then Carmen froze. She heard a sound.

A terrifying sound—the shuffling of footsteps behind her.

Carmen spun around and saw five huge, muscly men plodding up the corridor. They wore nothing but burlap shorts and some crude sandals. Their thick, curly hair was matted and dirty. Beneath their furrowed, protruding foreheads each thug had one long, black eyebrow; a big, ugly nose; and a thin-lipped mouth.

Carmen looked down at herself—she was still blending in perfectly with the white wall. Sighing with relief, she pressed herself flat against the wall. She stood very still as the thugs lumbered past her.

Carmen got a whiff as they walked by. She almost gagged.

Whew! she thought. *Somebody's* had sardines for lunch and hasn't had a bath in ages.

"We gonna be late to the lab," one of the thugs huffed in a deep, growly voice. "Can't make Sinus mad. Hurry!"

Well, well! Carmen thought. Talk about a short-cut. Sinus's thugs will lead me right to him.

As the thugs picked up speed, Carmen trotted along behind them. Using her gymnastics training, she stepped as lightly and silently as a cat. The thugs walked up, up, up the white corridor. Then they stopped and turned toward the blank white wall.

What're they doing? Carmen wondered.

Next, she heard a familiar, robotic voice pipe out of the wall.

"Security Brutes identified," the voice said. "Password?"

"Uhhhh, oh yeah, I remember," the lead brute replied. "Nose knows. Nose knows."

"Access—granted," the voice said. Then Carmen stifled a gasp as the white wall opened before the crowd of brutes. Without them, she might have walked these trick hallways forever! The brutes began to lumber through the opening.

Carmen knew the wall would snap closed as soon as the brutes passed through it. She had to make her move—now!

She dashed up the corridor and fell in step behind the last brute. But that wasn't close enough! The portal in the wall was closing right behind him. Carmen was going to be shut out. Or worse— trapped in the door as it clanked closed!

At the last instant, Carmen jumped onto the final thug's shoulders as he stepped through the door.

"Aaaaah!" the brute cried. He fell to his knees just as the portal closed behind him. It had worked—Carmen was in! She glanced around and saw that they were in a small, bare antechamber. Carmen jumped off the brute's shoulders and som- ersaulted over his head. Then she crouched in the chamber's corner and held her breath.

The thug jumped to his feet and looked wildly around the antechamber.

"Hey! Cut it out!" he cried to his comrades. "Someone pushed me!"

Carmen grinned as the security brutes began to scream at one another. They burst through a small door on the opposite side of the antechamber. Carmen silently followed them. As the brutes ran off, arguing, "No, *you* don't touch *me!*" Carmen gazed around the new room. Her eyes widened.

She was looking at an enormous, bustling laboratory. Everywhere she looked, beakers bubbled and test tubes tipped back and forth in robot-powered agitators. Scientists in white coats typed on computers. And a small army of security brutes stood against the walls.

In the middle of the lab was a raised platform. And sitting there, wearing a long white robe, was a man who could only have been Sinus.

The villain was impossibly tall and skinny. His skin was as white as powder. His head was as bald as a cue ball. His fingers were as long and trembly as spider legs. And his nose—well, it was the most hideous nose Carmen had ever seen. It was pink and sniffly and drippy.

Sinus was sitting in the center of a circular control panel. He was surrounded by flashing buttons and flickering video monitors and ominous cranks and levers. He'd been busily punching buttons and typing on a keyboard when the screaming brutes entered the lab. The villain glanced at the panicked security brutes. Then he clapped his hands.

"Silence," he cried. His voice was nasal and whiny and raspy. But it immediately quieted the thugs. They pressed their lipless mouths shut and trembled before their leader.

"What are you sniveling about?" Sinus shouted. "We have work to do!"

Then Sinus turned and looked straight at Carmen with evil, pink-rimmed eyes.

"Yes, we have lots of work to do—like getting rid of meddling spies," Sinus said.

Carmen gasped and looked down at her hands. *She could see them.* The Chameleo-Candy must have just worn off! Her cover was blown!

"So, *Spy Kid*," Sinus said. "You've decided to drop by. You should have phoned ahead."

Then he nodded ever so slightly at the security brutes stationed around the lab. They began to growl.

And ball up their fists.

Then they started stomping toward Carmen.

"As you can see," Sinus said in that horrible, wheezy voice of his, "my security brutes *really* don't like surprise visitors."

CHAPTER 8

As Juni watched Carmen tromp off through the brush, he turned to Maya.

"Okay," he said, "let's get one thing straight. I'm working with you to save the world, not because I trust you. 'Cause I don't."

"Well, you'd better," Maya said. "This is the jungle, Juni. It's rough-and-tumble out here. And the only people we have to rely on are each other."

"I'll rely on my wits, thank you very much," Juni said.

Creeeaaaaaaaak.

Juni looked around wildly.

"What's that noise?" he said.

"Sounds like splintering wood to me," Maya replied, examining her manicure with a bored expression.

CRACK!

Juni looked up to see the top of a palm tree—heading straight for him!

"Aaaaah!" he cried. The tree crashed to the ground, and Juni dove out of its way in the nick of time. He landed so hard, his spy watch flew off!

Plop.

The watch landed in a patch of sand about four feet away. And then—it began to sink.

"Quick Goo!" Juni shrieked. "No!"

He scrambled to the edge of the goo puddle and tried to make a grab for his spy watch. But in an instant, the watch had sunk into oblivion.

"Aw, man!" Juni said, lurching to his feet. "Now I have no way of reaching my parents *or* Carmen."

"Well," Maya said, hopping over the fallen palm tree to regard Juni. "At least you're alive."

"Don't sound so thrilled about it," Juni said. He wiped some dirt off his cargo pants. Then he began stomping down a trail, following the electrical cord Carmen had showed them.

"Let's follow this inland," he called to Maya.

Maya stomped behind him and said, "Well, who made you boss? I happen to think we should go in the opposite direction, toward the beach."

Juni skidded to a halt.

"You think Sinus would put his SNZ 100 on the beach?" he sputtered. "So any passing ship could just *see* it? I don't think so."

"Well," Maya said, "I do." She stuck out her chin stubbornly.

Juni stared hard at Maya. Then he spun around and continued walking inland. He'd find the SNZ 100 alone if that's how Maya felt about it.

But as he tromped down the trail, he could hear Maya following him.

Ha! Juni thought with a little smile. Victory!

Of course, he still had to find the SNZ 100. And walking all over the nose-shaped island could take hours and hours. Juni heaved a big sigh. Then, something occurred to him. He had lost his spy watch, but he *did* still have a beltful of gadgets! And one of those gadgets was the superextending periscope he'd snagged from the drill sub.

Juni snapped the thin brass tube from his belt and held the lens to his eye. Then he pressed a button. The periscope began to extend, and extend, and *extend* until it was wobbling in the breeze a hundred feet over Juni's head. He spun in a slow circle, checking out the terrain. Then he saw what he was looking for—a gap in the thick treetops.

Juni was *sure* that within that clearing, he'd find the SNZ 100—whatever it was. He touched a button on his periscope, and it retracted back into its tiny tube. Then he began hiking toward the clearing.

"Where are you going now?" Maya asked in exasperation.

"To the SNZ 100," Juni said. "I think it's about 250 yards northeast of us."

"Oh, please," Maya said, chasing after Juni. "What makes you think that?"

"There's a clearing in the jungle," Juni said over his shoulder. "It doesn't hurt to check it out."

"Well, it does if it wastes valuable time," Maya retorted. "And I think we should go this way." She pointed in the direction of the beach.

"Fine," Juni said. As he spoke, he extracted a chocolate energy bar from his vest pocket. All this arguing was making him hungry. "We will go that way . . ."

He watched Maya's shoulders sag with relief.

". . . just as soon as we've checked out my clearing," he added. He unwrapped his energy bar and started walking again. He was just about to bite into his snack when Maya grabbed him by the shoulder.

"I don't *think* so, Juni," she snarled. She spun him around roughly. So roughly, in fact, that Juni's energy bar flew out of his hand.

"My *snaaaaaccck!* Nooooooo!" he cried. He watched the chocolate hit another Quick Goo pit. It quickly disappeared.

Juni could live without his spy watch.

But his *food* was another matter entirely!

"Maya," Juni said through gritted teeth, "I'm onto you."

"I don't know what you mean," Maya said. She flung her long, silky hair over her shoulder with a sneer.

"You might have fooled Carmen, but you can't fool me—double agent!" Juni said.

"*What* did you call me?" Maya said. Her brown eyes widened.

"You've been trying to sabotage this mission from the start," Juni accused. In his head, it was all coming together. "You secretly stowed away on our drill sub. And you seem to have avoided getting shocked or gassed, even once! Almost as if you knew the lay of the land here on Mortille."

"Rubbish," Maya said.

"You sat there and watched while that falling tree practically squashed me," Juni continued. "And now you're trying to steer me away from the SNZ 100. *And* you're stealing all my food! Uncle Machete's hat was right—you're a liar!"

"You're simply bitter because you're just a klutzy ten-year-old," Maya said. "Face it, you'll never be the spy that Carmen is and you know it."

"That's not true," Juni said. "Me and Carmen are

a team. As if you know the meaning of the word."

"Oh, yeah?" Maya said. "Since when is a 'team-mate' jealous of his sister's friends?"

"Jealous?" Juni squeaked. "Ha!"

"Ha, yourself," Maya spat back.

"Well . . . ha-HA!" Juni retorted lamely.

And then there was nothing left for the two spies to do but glare at each other. And so they did—for a full thirty seconds.

Finally, Maya broke the angry silence.

"You want to do things your way, Juni?" she said. "Fine. But you'll do them alone."

She turned and stomped off into the jungle. In a few seconds, she had disappeared.

Juni harrumphed and returned to the trail he'd chosen earlier. He stomped through the jungle, muttering angrily.

"I'll . . . show her. . . ." he grumbled. "SNZ 100 . . . Sinus . . . double agent."

But the more Juni stomped and muttered, the worse he felt. He couldn't believe he'd revealed his suspicions to Maya. A good spy *never* shows his enemy what he's thinking.

Maya was right, Juni thought wanly—I *am* a klutz.

And she was right about another thing, too.

He was utterly alone.

The thought of it made Juni's feet get heavier. His head began to throb. He began to picture his mom's face. And all he wanted to do was run back to the drill sub.

But then, Juni shook his head.

"Being an OSS Spy means never giving up on a mission," he said to himself. "So, I'm going to find the SNZ 100! No matter wha—AHHHHHHHH!"

Juni had just glanced into the sky. And what he saw filled him with horror.

It was a fleet of planes. They were making a scraping, screeching noise.

Squaaaaaaawwwwwwwkkkkk!

Maybe they aren't planes, Juni thought. Maybe they're birds.

SQUAAWWWK!

The things swooped down further. And that's when Juni realized that they were planes *and* birds. They were huge, robotic parrots with glowing green eyes, foot-long, razor-sharp talons, and gnashing, knifelike beaks!

The robots—eight of them—circled above Juni, squawking angrily.

And then they began to zoom downward.

Juni dropped to the ground in terror.

The parrots were going to attack him!

CHAPTER 9

Juni cowered.

Then he cringed.

Then he screamed as one of the huge, vicious, robotic parrots began to lunge at him.

But finally, his spy instincts took over.

Since he was already flat on the ground, he quickly rolled into some nearby foliage. In an instant, he was buried in tangled vines and leaves. There was no way the parrots could see him.

He patted his utility belt and made a quick mental checklist of his spy gadgets.

"Let's see," he muttered. "I've got the 'wet noodle,' the 'stingray,' and the 'flibbertigibbet.' But none of those are *quite* right."

Then he pulled one last gadget out of his belt and regarded it admiringly.

"Perfect," he said. He gazed at the forked twig strung with a powerful rubber band. "The slingshot. Simple, yet elegant. Works every time."

But what to shoot at the parrots? In this sandy mulch, there wasn't a single stone to be found. Juni patted his vest pockets until he felt a small cube beneath his palm.

"My Sooper-Stretch Chocolate Saltwater Taffy," Juni groaned. "It's perfect. I guess I'm *never* gonna get a snack today!"

Regretfully, he pulled out the candy and popped it into his mouth. He began chewing like mad. Just as Juni began to taste its sweetness, the taffy began to expand and stretch in his mouth. Normally, this would provide hours of candy-gnawing fun. Now, Juni simply sighed and spit the taffy into his palm. He stretched it into a big, floppy pancake. Then he rolled out from beneath the ground cover and waited for a parrot to spot him.

He didn't have to wait long. With a tremendous squawk and a creaky flapping of metal wings, one of the robot birds swooped into Juni's range. Its eyes glowed an evil green. It began to dive, its wings outstretched.

Juni placed the taffy into the slingshot and stretched its rubber band to its limit.

SPROINNNGGGG! went the slingshot.

Splat! went the taffy. It landed right where Juni

had aimed—over the parrot's electronic eyes. The robot was blinded!

It began squawking and flapping wildly.

And then, it went into a nosedive.

Squaaaawwwk-squaaaawwwk-craaassshh.

Juni covered his head as the parrot smashed into the ground, spraying him with nuts and bolts.

"Ha-ha!" Juni said, wiggling his slingshot at the decimated parrot. "Don't mess with the slingshot."

SQUAAAAAWK!

Juni looked up.

"Uh-oh," Juni rasped.

He'd sort of forgotten about the *other* parrots circling through the sky. There were seven of them. And they were all heading straight for him.

The only thing to do was—

"Run, Juni!"

Juni gasped and glanced up at the voice. Perched in a treetop about fifty yards away was . . . Maya! And it looked like she wanted to help.

"Climb this tree," Maya called down to him. "I have a plan."

"Oh, like I'm supposed to trust you?" Juni hollered.

"C'mon," Maya yelled. "Carmen's my friend. And you're Carmen's brother. Which makes you my friend. Sort of. Besides what choice do you have?"

Squaaaawwwwk!

Juni glanced over his shoulder. The small army of robot parrots was bearing down on him. They were getting closer every second.

"You make a good point," Juni said. He started sprinting through the brush. As he ran, he pulled a Magneto-Rope out of his belt.

"The island," Juni remembered Carmen saying in the drill sub, "is completely wired. Sinus has electrified one third of the trees."

"Let's just hope this isn't one of those trees!" Juni grunted. He hurled the rope up toward the top of Maya's tree.

It stuck! And Juni wasn't zapped!

"Yes!" he whispered. He grabbed the rope and quickly scaled the palm tree. Soon, he was perched just below Maya under a canopy of huge, fanlike leaves. He peeked out from beneath the leaves and bit his lip. The parrots had clearly seen him shinny up the tree trunk. They were circling the tree hungrily.

Juni coiled up his Magneto-Rope and looked at Maya.

"Okay," he said. "So what's your plan?"

"See this?" she said. She pointed at a tiny red button in the tree trunk. It looked much like a light switch flipped to the OFF position. Maya grabbed a vine and handed it to Juni. She gripped another vine in her own fist.

"When the time is just right," Maya said, "I'm going to flip this switch, which will turn this tree into a shocker. But before the tree can zap us, we're going to make like Tarzan and swing away. Of course, howling like Tarzan won't be necessary."

"I don't know, Maya," Juni said, clinging to his vine and gazing down at the jungle floor. It looked veerrrrry far away. "We must be about three hundred feet up. And what do you mean, 'When the time is right'?"

"Could you, for once, just do what I say?" Maya said brusquely. "After all, I *am* older than you!"

"Hey!" Juni said. "Listen, you . . ."

"Sorry, no time," Maya said lightly. "Here come our parrot friends."

And she was right. The robotic birds' eyes were flashing. And their wings were flapping. They were clustered together, flying straight for them. Another few yards and they were going to make a direct hit.

"Looks like the time is just about right," Maya

said. "One . . . two . . . *three*!"

In one graceful motion, she gave Juni a push, flipped the red switch, and jumped off the tree herself.

"Aaaaah-eeyaya-eeyaya-aaaaaahh!" Juni screamed as he swung through the air at the end of his vine. He peeked over his shoulder just in time to see six metal parrots collide with the palm tree. The now *shocking* palm tree. The instant they hit, the parrots began to spark.

And sizzle.

And sputter.

And finally, they crashed—flaming and squawking—to the jungle floor beneath them. They were toast—literally.

"Whoo-hoo!" Juni cried. He caught hold of a tree branch and lowered himself to the ground. Then he looked around for Maya.

She'd swung her vine over to a nearby cliff top and landed on top of it. She waved down at Juni and gave him the thumbs-up.

And then, Juni saw a shadow fall over her. Something was creeping up behind her! Juni gasped—it was another parrot!

Juni's heart sank as he did some quick math. He'd seen *eight* parrots in the initial attack. He'd taken out one with his taffy, and six had crashed into the tree. He'd forgotten all about the last parrot. And now, Maya was going to pay for it!

"Look out behind you!" Juni cried.

Maya cupped a hand behind her ear and shook her head. She couldn't hear him!

"Behind you, behind you!" Juni screamed, pointing and jumping up and down.

Maya spun around just in time to scream in horror as the parrot scooped her up in its giant beak.

And then, the robot took flight.

Maya screamed and kicked her legs as the bird flew over Juni's head. It was headed toward another tree about a hundred feet away. The parrot dropped Maya into the tree's feathery leaves, then flew off.

Juni waited for Maya to poke her head through the leaves and wave at him. She didn't.

So he cocked his ear and listened for her shouts. There were none.

Maya had disappeared!

Juni began to race toward the tree. He wondered what sort of horrible things were happening in the treetop. Maybe Sinus was in there, just waiting to ensnare an OSS spy. Or perhaps Maya was being devoured by baby robot parrots.

Juni didn't know. All he did know was that Maya had saved his life. It was his duty as an honorable spy to save hers.

"Hang on, Maya!" he cried. "I'm coming!"

Juni reached the tree and tossed his Magneto-Rope against it. Then he began to shinny up the trunk.

About halfway up the tree, Juni paused to rest his aching muscles. He glanced beneath him. The ground was *very* far away. And the tree was swaying in the breeze.

"Whoa!" Juni whispered, feeling a wave of dizziness rush through his head. "Big mistake."

Just think about saving Maya, he told himself: you have to save Maya. Which means you have no time for fear.

The thought gave Juni a surge of strength, and he began shinnying up the tree trunk again. In no time at all, he'd reached the top of the tree. He poked around.

"Maya?" he called. "Where are you!"

Suddenly, Juni found himself tumbling down a gooey tunnel—a tunnel cleverly disguised as a tree trunk! When Juni hit the bottom of the slick slide, he found himself staring at thick, golden bars. He look around in panic. He and

Maya had landed in a giant parrot cage!

Juni jumped to his feet.

"Don't worry, Maya!" he cried. "I'll get us out of . . . this?"

Juni's eyes bulged.

And his mouth popped open.

Because Maya seemed to be just fine. She was leaning casually against the bars of the cage, her arms crossed over her chest. She was even smiling. It was the most sinister smile Juni had ever seen.

What's more—Maya wasn't alone.

She was flanked by four, brooding, smelly brutes with unibrows and matted hair. They wore brown T-shirts and brown shorts. And they had lots of bulging muscles.

"Sinus's thugs!" Juni breathed.

"Actually, they're called 'security brutes,'" Maya said. "And believe me, you don't want to get these guys upset. They'll snap you like a twig."

"How do you know that?" Juni said in a trembling voice.

"How do I know?" Maya said with an evil laugh. "Because I live here on Mortille. And guess what, Juni? As of today—so do you!"

CHAPTER 10

Carmen was standing in Sinus's laboratory—the center of his evil empire. Her fists were clenched, and her legs were as tense as coiled springs. She looked totally tough. But inside—she was bumming.

Talk about amazingly bad timing, she thought. My Chameleo-Candy *had* to wear off just as I walked in on the evil Sinus and his crew of disgusting brutes.

"So what will it be, Spy Kid?" Sinus was asking her. His voice was so whiny-raspy-nasty that Carmen couldn't help but cringe as he spoke. "Will you let me go about my business? Or do you want to go up against my big, strong brutes?"

Carmen glanced around Sinus's control room, counting the thugs that surrounded him. There were ten of them.

That was a *bunch* of brutes.

Carmen thought hard. And then . . . she

unclenched her fists and dropped her hands. Her shoulders slumped, and her chin dropped to her chest in shame.

She surrendered.

"I thought you'd see it my way," Sinus cackled. "Lock her up, my brutes. I'll wait in my office. Let me know when she's behind bars!"

As Sinus shuffled toward the control room door, Carmen slumped even further. She looked utterly defeated. Two brutes lumbered over. They grabbed her hands and started to drag her away. But at the last moment, she dug in her heels.

"Sinus," Carmen said to the supervillain's back. "Before they take me away, I just want to say one thing."

Sinus turned around with a simpering smile and nodded.

"I'll allow that," he said.

"When you decided to mess with Carmen Cortez," she announced, "you made a *big* mistake."

Carmen ripped her arms out of the thugs' clumsy fists and pulled the hair on their hairy arms.

"Aaaaiggh!" the brutes screamed. Then Carmen elbowed both thugs in the stomach, sending them flying.

When Sinus finally recovered from his shock, he screeched at his remaining brutes.

"Get her!" he ordered.

That's when Carmen *really* got busy. Her arms and legs whirled like pinwheels as she kicked this brute in the chin and that one in the gut.

All *right*, Carmen thought, as she fought brute after brute. I've conquered more of these hairy thugs than I can count. And it looks like I only have . . .

Carmen took a quick survey of the control room.

. . . four to go! she thought. If this is all there is, I can totally take them.

But then, Carmen's heart sank.

Because that *wasn't* all there was. In fact, a whole new crew of security brutes—dozens of them— were lumbering into the lab at that very moment.

Carmen's face fell.

"Stop it!" she screamed at the stream of thugs. "Stay away! Or I'll . . . I'll . . ."

"You'll what?" said a voice. A familiar voice. It was coming from the end of the line of brutes.

"Maya?" Carmen said.

It *was* Maya. She leaped into the control room and gave Carmen a thumbs-up.

"You got it!" Maya said. "Let's beat these stinky thugs together, friend."

Carmen grinned, and she felt a new wave of energy surge into her limbs. She began kicking, punching, and pounding the brutes anew. Maya was right by her side, punching and kicking, too.

See, Carmen thought, this is what being best friends/spies is all about—watching out for each other!

Speaking of . . .

"Maya," Carmen shrieked as she saw a thug lunging at her friend. "Watch out for that brute!"

Maya ducked just in time to avoid a hammy fist to the head. She popped up and grinned at Carmen.

"Thanks," she said. Then her mouth popped open, and she pointed over Carmen's shoulder.

"Uh-oh," she cried. "Now *you'd* better watch it!"

Carmen jumped up and spun around. But there was nobody behind her.

"What?" she said in bewilderment. She spun around again. And that's when she got *really* confused.

Maya was standing within the crowd of brutes. But none of them was grabbing at her. Or punching her.

In fact, they were looking at her expectantly. Almost as if they were waiting for Maya to give them an order.

And that's just what she did.

"Grab her, brutes," she barked.

"What?" Carmen sputtered. She was so shocked,

she went limp. And before she knew it, six of the thugs had seized her by every limb. She flailed and struggled but there were too many of them. She'd been defeated.

Make that—betrayed!

"Maya!" Carmen said. "Why, why are you doing this?"

"Hel-lo?" Maya said. "Do the words 'world domination' mean anything to you?"

"No," Carmen spat. "That's Sinus's plan, not yours."

"Well, since Sinus is my father," Maya said, "I'd say it's a family affair, wouldn't you?"

"What?" Carmen screamed. "Ew!"

"Relax," Maya said dryly. "I'm adopted. It's true, what I told you about my being an orphan. But it wasn't the OSS that took me in. It was Sinus. Talk about being the luckiest girl in the world."

"You can't really care about Sinus and his crazy plan!" Carmen said to Maya desperately. "You don't mean that."

"Oh, I do," Maya said. "And I mean this, too."

Maya clapped her hands and addressed the brutes pinning down Carmen's arms and legs.

"Security Brutes?" she said. "Let me introduce you to Carmen Cortez. Lock her up!"

The brutes dragged Carmen back down the long, curvy corridor. Behind her, she could hear Maya chuckling with satisfaction.

And before Carmen knew it, she was being hauled up to a small electronic door. Maya slipped in front of them and placed her palm on a rectangular sensor next to the door. The sensor glowed bright green as it read her fingerprints. Then the door whooshed open, and the brutes pushed Carmen through it.

She landed in a bare white cell. There was nothing in the room except two sets of titanium wrist and ankle cuffs protruding from the wall.

One set of cuffs was empty.

And in the other . . .

"Juni!" Carmen screamed.

Carmen's little brother was strapped to the wall. His feet dangled about two feet off the floor. His arms were clamped to the wall over his head.

And it was all Carmen's fault.

"You were right about Maya," Carmen said. "I'm sorry."

"It's gonna be okay," Juni said. But Carmen could see that Juni's eyes were filled with fear.

Maya stepped into the cell and snapped her fingers at a crowd of brutes.

"What are you waiting for?" she said. "Cuff her!"

Carmen put up her dukes, but just as quickly as before, the security brutes ganged up on her. Before she knew it, they'd pushed her up against the wall next to Juni.

Maya strolled to a control panel next to the door and pushed a few buttons. The shiny silver cuffs came to life and clamped themselves around Carmen's ankles and wrists.

Now she was trapped, too.

There was nothing either of the Spy Kids could do except glare at Maya—their double-crosser.

"Why'd you do it, Maya?" Juni asked. "What do you have to gain by teaming up with Sinus?"

"Oh, I don't know," Maya said snidely. "Becoming princess of the world, perhaps."

"Yeah, *evil* princess of the world," Carmen said.

"Details, details," Maya said with a yawn. "Listen, some of us get to grow up in nice, cozy, cliff top mansions with dads who speak Spanish and moms who are really rad. And some of us are poor, little orphans. It just doesn't seem fair, does it?"

"You're right," Carmen said. "It's *not* fair. But,

Maya, that's no reason to destroy every satellite in the world!"

"Oh, but it is," Maya said. "I lost my parents— but I've gained world domination. I think that's a *sweet* deal."

"You'll never get away with it," Juni said.

"Actually, I will," Maya said. "And the funny thing is, you'll be right where I was. Poor. Powerless. And parentless."

Carmen felt a chill shoot through her.

"*What* . . . did . . . you . . . just . . . say?" she growled at Maya. Her wrists grated against their titanium cuffs. She was just itching to get at her "friend."

"Remember my little 'bathroom break' when we first got to the island?" Maya asked. She paced back and forth between Juni and Carmen, smiling tauntingly at them.

"What about it?" Juni said.

"I was actually busy putting a sucker lock on the drill sub," Maya said. "With your parents inside."

"No!" Juni yelled.

"You . . . you didn't," Carmen whispered.

"I did," Maya said. "And we all know what a sucker lock does, don't we? It's a brilliant gadget, I must say. It starts off as a little ball of sticky, gunky stuff—like putty or paste. But put it, say, onto the door of a submarine and the ball of gunk expands. And expands. Until it covers the vehicle entirely."

"No . . ." Juni groaned.

"Yes," Maya said with a grin. "The sucker lock seals the sub up tight. Radio contact is broken. Nobody gets out. And nobody gets in. Until . . ."

"Until . . ." Carmen said. Her lower lip was quivering.

"Until, four hours after deployment, the sucker lock explodes," Maya stated, "destroying everything it touches. And in this case, that would be Gregorio and Ingrid Cortez. Loving parents. Former superspies. Poof!"

There was nothing more that Carmen and Juni could say. Juni trembled with rage and Carmen stared at Maya with dark, sad eyes.

But Maya couldn't have cared less. She glanced at her watch. "Oops," she said. "Only two hours before Mommy and Daddy go boom."

Then she flipped her glossy hair over her shoulder and turned on her heel to flounce out of the cell. But before she was through the door, she paused and peeked over her shoulder.

"No one can stop me and Sinus now," she announced. "Oh, and Carmen?"

"What?" Carmen growled.

"Thanks for the sleepover," Maya said. "It was *ever* so much fun."

Then she winked and stepped through the door. It whooshed shut behind her.

Carmen and Juni were imprisoned.

Their parents were sitting ducks.

And Juni's suspicion was finally proved—Maya Sinclair had completely duped them.

CHAPTER 11

For a moment, Carmen and Juni simply hung from the wall in silence.

Carmen dropped her head in shame.

The OSS trusted me, she thought. Not to mention my family. I've failed them all.

"No, you didn't," Juni said.

Carmen looked up in surprise.

"What?" she said. "I didn't say anything."

"You didn't have to," Juni said, gazing at her sadly. "I know what you're thinking. You're thinking that you believed Maya and that's what got us here."

"I . . ." Carmen stuttered. "I—"

"It's not your fault," Juni said. "You wanted her to be your friend. It's totally understandable."

Carmen smiled at her brother.

"Thanks, Juni," she whispered.

"There's something else," Juni said.

"Yeah?"

"My tooth's really loose," Juni said. He opened

his mouth and wiggled the tooth—the one just to the right of his front teeth—with his tongue. "I think it's about to fall out."

"Um, Juni," Carmen said, "that's great and all. But shouldn't we be worrying about saving ourselves, our parents, and the world? The tooth fairy's gonna have to wait."

"Actually, this tooth *could* save us," Juni said.

With that, Juni began to concentrate on his loose tooth. He pushed at it with the tip of his tongue. He wiggled it and waggled it and shoved it around until he heard a little pop. The next thing he knew, the tooth was swimming around in his mouth.

Then Juni pursed his lips.

And he squinted at the control panel by the cell door.

Finally, he took a deep breath—and spat!

"What are you—?" Carmen cried.

But Juni barely heard her. He was watching his tooth fly through the air. His aim was perfect.

Doink.

The tooth hit one of the buttons on the control panel! Then, with a breathy *shooooosh,* two of Carmen's titanium cuffs popped open. Her right arm and right leg were freed!

"Juni!" Carmen said. "You're brilliant!"

"I'm going to remember you said that!" Juni replied with a gap-toothed grin. Then his smile quickly faded away.

"Too bad I don't have any more loose teeth," he said. "Lot of good it does us to have only two of your limbs free."

"Wait a minute," Carmen said. "I have an idea."

With her free hand, she unzipped one of her vest pockets and pulled out a piece of Chameleo-Candy. She popped it out of its wrapper and into her mouth. She winced. This time the candy tasted like salty licorice. Blech!

But at least the candy worked! Within a few seconds, Carmen's clothes and skin had gone as white as the cell wall. She was invisible.

"Ahh!" Juni shrieked. "Carmen! Where'd you go?"

"Shhh," Carmen hissed. "I'm still here. I ate some of Uncle Machete's Chameleo-Candy."

"Cool," Juni breathed.

"But that's only half the plan," Carmen said. "You need to be invisible, too. Catch."

Carmen reached into her pocket and pulled out her last piece of Chameleo-Candy. She was just about to toss it to Juni when it slipped from her fingers!

"Oh, no!" Carmen shrieked.

Instinctively, she thrust her foot out. And despite the fact that her foot was invisible, she managed to catch the candy on the toe of her boot. She balanced the sweet on it as if it were a Hacky Sack. Then, very carefully, she spoke.

"Juni," she said quietly. "This is the last piece of candy. As in—our last chance."

"I understand," Juni said. "Hit me!"

Carmen flipped the candy off her toe. Then she bounced it with her knee and sent it sailing over to her brother.

Juni opened his mouth wide and snapped his teeth over the candy. He'd caught it!

Juni spit out the Chameleo-Candy's wrapper and began chewing madly. Then he made a horrible face.

"Ugh," he said. "What's in this candy? Actual chameleons? It tastes like burnt brussels sprouts."

"Keep chewing," Carmen ordered him.

Juni swallowed the candy with a gagging noise. Then he faded away before Carmen's very eyes.

"You there?" she whispered.

"Yup," Juni's disembodied voice said.

"Okay," Carmen said. "Now all we have to do is hope someone comes in before the candy wears off."

"How long does *that* take?" Juni said.

"Well, last time, it took about twenty minutes," Carmen said.

"Aw, man!" Juni started to complain. But Carmen shushed him when she heard a shuffling noise outside their cell.

"Quiet!" she said. "Someone's coming."

No sooner had the words left her mouth than the cell door whooshed open. A very large and pudgy thug lumbered in.

It took a moment for the blank-eyed brute to realize the prisoners had disappeared. But finally, he noticed Juni's seemingly empty cuffs. Then he saw Carmen's. And then the thug's beady eyes bulged.

Come on over, Carmen thought. Take a closer look. That's right . . .

As if he'd heard Carmen's silent order, the brute stumbled forward. His mouth puckered into a confused frown, and his unibrow twitched nervously.

"Escaped," the brute said in a raspy voice. He was peering at Carmen's open cuffs in confusion. "Maya's gonna be real mad."

You bet she is, Carmen thought. Now come just a liiiiittle closer.

Finally, the brute stepped into Carmen's range.

He was reaching toward her open wrist cuff.

And *that's* when Carmen grabbed the brute by his dirty hair.

"Boo!" Carmen yelled.

The brute began shaking in fear. Carmen spun him around and grabbed his meaty shoulder. She planted the sole of her boot squarely in the middle of his back and gave a mighty kick.

The bellowing brute went flying across the room. And he didn't stop until he hit the wall.

Make that the *control panel* in the wall. The brute's big, round belly smashed into the panel, pressing a multitude of buttons all at once.

Shoosh. Shoosh. Shoosh. Shoosh. Shoosh. Shoosh.

Carmen's two remaining cuffs sprang open, and all four of Juni's cuffs unlocked! The titanium loops retracted into the wall. Carmen dropped to the floor with a thump. She heard another thump and knew that Juni had fallen as well.

They were free!

"Follow me," Carmen whispered to Juni as the guard continued to screech in terror.

"How?" Juni whispered back. "I can't see you!"

"Oh, yeah," Carmen said. "Okay, dash out the door and turn right."

The invisible Spy Kids inched around the

hysterical thug and began racing down a long corridor. When the hallway forked, Carmen skidded to
a stop.

"Ooooff!" Juni grunted as he crashed into her.

"Ugh!" Carmen said. "Watch where you're
going, Juni!"

"Hel-lo?," Juni said. "I am. There's nothing to
see, chameleon. Anyway, I think we should take the
left fork."

"No, I'm pretty sure it's the right," Carmen said.

"How would you know?" Juni challenged.

"Well, how would you?" Carmen shot back.
She wrung her invisible hands. "Oh, if only we
could reach Mom and Dad. They'd be able to see
our location from the bugs I planted. They'd
guide us out."

"Carmen?" Juni said softly. "What if we never
reach Mom and Dad again?"

"Don't say that!" Carmen said. "We're going to
save them."

"If we ever get out of here," Juni said morosely.

"We will," Carmen said. "We'll take the left fork.
Let's just hope you're right."

"You mean left," Juni said.

"Right," Carmen said. Then she shook her
head. "I mean correct!"

Carmen heard her brother snort with laughter.

"You had *better* not be sticking your tongue out at me," Carmen said.

"You'll never know," Juni teased. "Okay, let's get going."

The Spy Kids veered left. The bright, white corridor sloped upward for a while. Then it went down. Then it angled to the left, then right, then right again. Then it spiraled wildly.

"This can't be right," Carmen finally cried in frustration.

"Well, we've come this far," Juni said. "It's got to lead *somewhere*. Let's keep going."

And Juni was right. Only a couple of twists and turns later, a doorway appeared. Luckily, there was a window in the door. Juni was too short to see through it, but if Carmen stood on her tiptoes, she could just peek inside.

"Oh, no," she complained. "This is just the kitchen."

"The kitchen?" Juni's stomach rumbled.

"C'mon, Juni," Carmen said. "This is no time for a snack."

She looked around the kitchen. There was nothing else to see except lots of brutes cooking, cleaning, and hauling garbage out the back door.

Hey, wait a minute, Carmen suddenly realized. *The back door!*

"There's a back door!" Carmen squeaked to Juni. "This is our way out of the Ol-Factory. We just have to sneak by all those brutes."

"No problem," Juni said, looking down at his arm. It was covered in the same black-and-white speckles as the linoleum floor. "We're still blending."

"Okay," Carmen said, taking another peek. "The brutes seem immersed in their work. Just be completely silent and they won't see us."

"Right," Juni said. "I mean, correct."

Then Juni started to giggle.

"Juniiiii," Carmen whispered threateningly.

"Okay, okay," Juni said, stifling one final snort. "I'm ready."

Carmen gently pushed the door open and slipped inside the kitchen. She felt Juni sneak in behind her.

They began to tiptoe across the kitchen. There was a clear pathway to the door.

This is going to be a piece of cake, Juni thought.

Then a fabulous aroma wafted beneath his nose.

Hey, he thought woozily. I *smell* a piece of cake. He glanced to his left. A brimming tray of food was only inches from his elbow. And there, on the tray's corner, was a creamy, fluffy, toasty-smelling piece of coconut shortcake.

Juni felt his mouth water and his stomach gurgle.

He'd lost his meatball hero and chocolate energy bar. And his saltwater taffy.

He hadn't had a snack for *hours.*

And before Juni could think twice about it, he'd filched the cake from the tray.

Just one little bite, he thought, and I'll put the rest back.

Of course, Juni didn't count on one of the brutes seeing him grab the cake. Or rather, seeing a piece of cake seem to levitate in the air, all by itself. He was still invisible, after all.

But one of the brutes saw it, indeed. The thug pointed at the floating pastry in horror. And then he began to shout!

Every other brute in the kitchen spun around and saw the "floating cake" as well.

That's when bedlam broke out.

Carmen had almost reached the kitchen's back door when she heard the commotion. She spun around and saw the thugs wailing and pointing at a piece of floating coconut cake. A piece that was slowly disappearing, bite by bite.

"Juni!" she yelled.

The brutes jumped and turned toward her voice. When they realized the voice had come from some invisible source, they started shouting some more.

"They're gonna blow our cover!" Carmen cried.

"Only one more bite," Juni protested. He was just bringing the delicious coconut cake to his invisible lips when something happened.

Juni's hand, clutching the fluffy cake, appeared before his eyes. Then came his arm. And his shirt. And his legs. And finally his sheepish face, gazing at the crowd of brutes.

And the fear in the thugs' eyes? Well, *that* was disappearing.

"That Maya's prisoner!" one of the brutes grunted.

"Guys, guys," Juni said, tossing the last bit of cake back on the tray. He backed away slowly. "Can we talk about this?"

"We don't care what you say," a brute replied, shrugging his beefy shoulders. "We pound you, anyway."

"Well, then I say, 'Sproing,'" Juni said with a glint in his eyes. He bent over and reached for his spy boots.

"Sproing?" the brutes said.

"Sproing?" Carmen said.

Sproing! Juni activated the springs in his spy boot soles! Waving at the brutes with his frosting-covered fingers, he suddenly bounced over their heads, sailed across the kitchen, and landed next to his sister.

Carmen and Juni looked at each other. Then they looked at the advancing brutes.

"Sproing?" Juni said.

"Sproing!" Carmen said with a quick nod. She activated her own spring soles. Then the Spy Kids spun around and bounced out of the Ol-Factory. They sailed straight into the thick jungle foliage and disappeared from the brutes' view.

"Oooof!" Carmen said as she landed on a narrow trail. She quickly stuffed her springs back into her spy boots and hopped to her feet.

Juni landed in a patch of foliage with a grunt. Both kids ducked down and listened for the brutes. But clearly, their quick exit had left the thugs flummoxed. They didn't even know where to begin chasing the Spy Kids down.

Juni crawled out of the dense weeds. "That was a close one," Juni said. "Really good cake, though!"

Carmen glared at him.

"I'll deal with you later," Carmen said. "*After* we rescue Mom and Dad."

"Right," Juni said, scratching at his arm vigorously.

"Let's see," Carmen said, glancing at the sun and then adjusting the compass in her spy watch. "The drill sub should be north by northeast. . . ."

Scritch, scritch, scritch.

Juni was scratching his leg now. And then a spot on his neck. Carmen paused in her calculations and stared at her brother. Big red bumps were forming all over his arms and legs. Then she looked at the patch of weeds in which he'd landed.

"Juni!" she suddenly cried. "It's the mutant poison ivy. Don't touch those bumps!"

"I have to!" Juni cried. "They itch like mad."

Carmen looked at her spy watch and saw that an hour had gone by since Maya had locked them in the cell.

"Juni?" she said. "We don't have much time left before the sucker lock explodes. So you have to stop scratching and start *running*."

CHAPTER 12

Carmen and Juni whipped out their auto weed whackers and began desperately hacking their way through the jungle.

"So, uh," Juni began as he tromped along behind his sister, "how should we dismantle the sucker lock. Any ideas?"

Carmen thought hard as she whacked elephant ears and palm fronds out of her way. And then, her shoulders sagged.

"No," she admitted. "The sucker lock is one of the most ingenious gadgets ever invented. It's got no fuse. No computer. No seams. It's perfect."

"Perfectly evil," Juni agreed.

"We'll figure something out," Carmen said roughly. "We have to. But first we have to get there."

The kids picked up their speed, tearing up the foliage. They thought only of their parents. And the minutes of their parents' lives—ticking away.

"We're almost there," Carmen said, after several

minutes of hacking. "Just keep going."

"Oka-AAAAAAYYYYYY!" Juni cried. His foot had just slipped into something next to the trail. Something soft. And gooey. And squishy. And sucking.

"Quick Goooooo!" Juni cried.

In a few seconds, the Quick Goo puddle swallowed Juni's entire leg. The snotty stuff yanked at him so hard, his other leg was dragged in, too.

"Carmen!" he yelled, holding his arms over his head. *Help!*

Carmen dropped her auto weed whacker and felt for a hidden button on her spy vest. She pushed it with all her strength.

A long, thin cable shot out of her vest, unfurling with a *zinging* noise until it landed in the Quick Goo next to Juni.

"Grab the cable!" she screamed.

Juni scooped the thin cable out of the goo and hung on as Carmen braced her feet and pushed the RETRACT button in her vest.

But Juni's hands were covered with goo. They were too slippery! The cable slipped right through his fingers.

"Now, what?" Juni said. "Carmen, save . . . glub! *Glub-glub. GLUB!*"

Juni's mouth had just dipped into the Quick

Goo. His nose was next. Which meant Carmen had only seconds to come up with a plan.

"What's the stickiest substance on earth?" she asked herself. She stared at her brother's hands, anxiously flapping out of the Quick Goo. Suddenly, she knew the answer—Fooglie Fruit Punch!

Carmen ripped her canteen out of her utility belt. She poured her Kumquat-Kiwi punch all over the cable. Then she tossed it to Juni again. He made a grab for the rope and held on tight.

And this time, when Carmen pushed the RETRACT button, Juni's hands stuck. He slithered out of the Quick Goo pit and crawled, hacking and coughing, over to his sister.

"Juni!" Carmen cried, putting her hands on his gooey shoulders. "Are you okay?"

"Yeah." Juni huffed, stumbling to his feet. "Just give me . . . a minute . . . to catch . . . my breath."

He staggered over to a palm tree and leaned against it heavily.

That's when the Spy Kids heard the telltale sound of an impending shock.

Ssssszzzzzz.

"Watch out," Carmen cried. "It's gonna shock you!"

But, to Juni's surprise, the shock never came!

The tree only made a limp, sizzling noise. Then it sagged a little, as if it had shorted out.

"Huh?" Carmen said. She walked over to the tree and put one of her hands—still slick with Quick Goo—on the trunk. The tree made another halfhearted sizzle. Then it sagged again.

"I wonder why," Carmen said, leaning against the tree with her elbow, "this one didn't shock us."

Zzzzzttttt!

"Ow!" Carmen screamed. She jumped away from the tree and blew a puff of smoke off her freshly shocked elbow.

Then she and Juni stared at each other, wide-eyed.

"The goo!" they said at the same time.

Juni felt strength snap back into his limbs. He snatched Carmen's empty canteen from the ground where she'd dropped it. Then he inched carefully over to the edge of the Quick Goo pit and dipped the canteen in, filling it with the green, slimy stuff. Capping the canteen, Juni scooped up an extra handful and slapped it on his neck.

"This Quick Goo also seems to stop the bumps from itching," he said to Carmen. "Bonus!"

"Let's just hope it works as well for Mom and Dad," she cried.

Then she picked up her auto weed whacker and returned to hacking through the jungle. The Spy Kids plowed through the jungle, breathing hard, until finally, they skidded to a halt.

They'd arrived at the drill sub.

The swoosh-shaped vehicle was encased in a thick layer of sticky, rubbery purple stuff—the sucker lock.

"Mom, Dad?" Carmen called as Juni ran up beside her. "We're here. Can you hear us?"

But the only response Carmen got was the sound of her own voice, echoing back through the eerily, silent jungle.

Carmen and Juni looked at each other.

But suddenly, they heard something. They turned back to the drill sub hopefully. And then, they both went pale.

The sound they'd heard was a smoky sizzle. Not to mention, an ominous popping.

And that smell they were suddenly noticing? It was the bitter scent of burning rubber.

And that cloudy stuff they were suddenly seeing? That was an early plume of smoke, wafting off the sucker lock.

"It's gonna blow!" Carmen screamed.

CHAPTER 13

"It's *not* going to blow," Juni yelled, looking at the smoking sucker lock defiantly. "Not if I can help it!"

He dashed back to the trail and scooped the canteen up from the ground. Then he ran over to the sucker-locked sub and began slapping the goo wherever he saw a plume of smoke.

"Lemme help!" Carmen cried. She ran up to Juni and held out her hand. Juni dumped some Quick Goo into her palm. They began smearing the gross, green stuff all over the sucker lock.

When they'd completely covered the craft with Quick Goo, they stumbled backward. Then they waited.

And waited.

Until finally, one by one, the little plumes of smoke fizzled out.

The popping noises of an impending explosion pooped out.

And the sizzling sound stopped altogether.

"It worked!" Juni breathed.

"And hey, look," Carmen said. She pointed at an empty patch in the sucker lock. The invisible drill sub was peeking through the purple shell! "I think the goo is melting the sucker lock away."

She was right. The purple, rubbery stuff was rapidly disappearing. Before Carmen and Juni knew it, they were blinking at a seemingly empty clearing—the unsuckered, invisible drill sub.

They ran up to the point where they knew the sub's hatch lay and began banging on the door, calling out their parents' names. With a loud *hissssssss*, the hatch opened. Mom and Dad poked their heads out, holding OSS-issued ray guns.

When they saw Carmen and Juni, they dropped their weapons and leaped out of the drill sub.

"Oh, kids!" Mom cried. She scooped them up into a huge hug.

"We were so worried about you!" Dad said, joining the group squeeze.

"About *us*?" Juni exclaimed. "You were the ones trapped inside a smoking sucker lock."

"Well, uh," Dad said with a shrug, "yes, we were a little worried about that, too."

"But we knew our Spy Kids would save us," Mom said. She kissed Juni on top of his wet, gooey head.

"Ew, Juni, what's this sticky stuff all over you?"

"Trust me, Mom," he said, "you don't want to know."

"But we *do* want to know how we're going to save the day," Carmen said. "Did you get any feedback from the bugs I planted?"

"Not a speck," Mom said. "Sinus's sucker lock blocked all transmissions."

"Um, Mom," Carmen said. She heaved a big sigh and looked at her feet. "There's something I have to tell you. It wasn't just Sinus's sucker lock. It was Maya's, too. She's in with the bad guys. Juni was right. And . . . I'm so sorry!"

"We figured as much," Dad said, stroking his daughter's tangled curls. "It's okay, Carmenita. We were taken in, too. Maya's a very good double agent. But she won't succeed."

"How do you know?" Carmen asked. Her voice was raspy and tear-choked.

"Because she's alone," Dad said. "And we Cortezes—we have each other."

Carmen threw herself into her father's arms.

Krrrrgggh!

A staticky noise from the drill sub interrupted the family reunion. The Cortezes ran to the sub's hatch and cocked their ears.

"Roger," said a voice in the drill sub's computer. "We're readying the SNZ 100 for deployment now. We simply have to rotate it into alignment with the satellites in outer space. It should take about an hour."

"Perfect," purred a whiny, nasal voice.

"That's Sinus!" Carmen said. "I'd know that voice anywhere. The bugs I planted must be transmitting now that the sucker lock is gone!"

"Our Spy Kids may have escaped." Sinus's voice hissed in the computer. "But they won't have time to squelch the Big Sneeze. Only one hour till my beautiful SNZ 100 goes, 'Achoo!'"

And then Sinus's maniacal laughter echoed out of the drill sub.

With that, the Cortezes sprang to action.

"That madman thinks he can take my children prisoner and then just go, 'Achoo'?" Dad said. "I don't think so! We will find this SNZ 100 and take it out. Now, we could separate and cover the island more quickly. . . ."

"You know, Dad?" Carmen interrupted. "I think we'd be better off if we stuck together. As a spy team."

"As a family," Juni added.

"I think that's an excellent suggestion," Mom said with a warm smile.

"And you know . . ." Juni said, putting a slimy fist to his slimy chin. "I just realized something. I think I know where the SNZ 100 is!"

"You do?" Carmen exclaimed. "How?"

"When I was hunting with Maya, I saw a clearing in the jungle," Juni said. "I wanted to check it out, but she was dead set against it. She was desperate to hide something."

"I guess she didn't know how good we are at playing hide-and-seek," Carmen said. "Let's move."

With Juni in the lead, the Cortezes tramped through the jungle. The Spy Kids taught their parents how to recognize the telltale crackle of a shocking tree and step around mushroom gas-passers. They warned them about the Quick Goo pits and mutant poison ivy. Then Juni told them about his battle with the robotic parrots.

"Junito," Dad said. "I'm so proud of you! You've got Sinus's evil schemes all figured out."

Ssssssssssss-ZOT!

The family skidded to a halt as a shower of sparks flew out of a nearby palm tree. Then a flaming coconut shot out from beneath the palm fronds and headed straight for Dad!

"Whoa!" he yelled. He leaped out of the way as

the coconut landed with a loud boom—right where he'd been standing.

"Gregorio," Mom groaned. "You *know* Regulation C-22—the Jinx Code."

"Never declare a victory mid-mission," Dad remembered, snapping his fingers in annoyance. "How could I forget?"

Ssssssss-ZOT! Ssssssss-ZOT!

Dozens of palm trees had begun sparking and lobbing coconut grenades at the family. Dad rolled to one side of the trail and ducked beneath a shrub. Mom, Carmen, and Juni dove to the other side of the trail. They peeked out at Dad from beneath some thick foliage.

"Sorry, kids," Dad said from beneath the leafy branches. "At least we know everything that Sinus is throwing at us now, eh?"

"Jinx!" Carmen and Juni cried as Dad clapped a hand over his mouth.

And sure enough, an enormous, echoing belch suddenly filled the air. Trembling, the spies peeked out of their hiding places to find the source of the sound.

"I think it's coming from that mountain," Carmen said. She pointed at a steep hill about a half mile away.

"I don't think that's a mountain," Mom said, as the hill unleashed another bellowing burp. Next, a great geyser of glowing, green slop shot out of its peak.

"You're right," Dad said. "It's a volcano!"

"And that's no lava," Juni shouted as the neon-green goo began to slither down the hillside. Everything in its path—from palm trees to boulders—melted into sizzling puddles.

"It's acid!" Juni shouted. "Run!"

Creeeak-SQUAAAAAWK!

The Cortezes gasped and looked up.

A fleet of robotic parrots was bearing down on them from the sky.

The spies gave one another a quick, alarmed glance.

"Jet shoes?" Dad mouthed at his family.

Carmen, Juni, and Mom nodded vigorously.

Dad held up three fingers . . . two fingers . . . ONE!

Shwoooooooosssssshhhh!

With a yank of their bootlaces, the Cortezes' shoes began to spit out fire. An instant later, each spy shot into the air.

"Watch the parrots, kids!" Mom called as Carmen and Juni swooped through the air like trapeze artists. They flew so fast, they were nothing but blurs.

"Follow me!" Juni called. He jetted over to a palm tree with a long umbrella of feathery leaves. He poked his finger through the leaves and quickly found a red ON/OFF switch. He flicked it to OFF, then clung to the de-shocked trunk as Carmen and his parents landed below him. They clustered together so the palm leaves completely hid them.

"Okay," Carmen whispered desperately. "We're dealing with robotic parrots, coconut bombs, and an acid-spewing volcano. Suggestions?"

"Solution!" Juni said, reaching into his spy vest. He pulled out a slim booklet and waved it at his bewildered family members. "This is going to save our butts!"

"What is it?" Carmen blurted.

Dad took the booklet from Juni and read its title: "*Gadgetry and the Great Outdoors* by Machete Cortez. It's a guide to building high-grade gizmos out of anything you might find in the wild—coconuts, palm leaves, tree bark, even sand."

"I found it in the box of gadgets Uncle Machete sent," Juni said with a shrug.

"Good job," Mom said. "Now, I estimate we have, oh, ten minutes before Sinus sniffs us out. So, grab whatever natural resource you can find and get busy. It's world-saving time. Now or never!"

CHAPTER 14

Just as Mom had predicted, it didn't take long for the enemy to find the Cortezes' palm tree. A few minutes after the spies had landed, robotic parrots began circling the treetop like vultures. Sizzling coconuts zinged over from neighboring trees. And a stream of volcanic acid inched ever closer.

On the bright side, the Spy family had a plan.

A plan that would rest on the shoulders of one Cortez.

Now, all they had to do was decide which Cortez that would be.

"Of course, I will do it," Dad declared. "That is what dads do."

"Dad," Carmen said gently. "You're too big. This is a job only a Spy Kid can do. And that Spy Kid should be me."

"She's right, Gregorio," Mom said softly.

"All right," Dad relented. Then he looked at Carmen. "But remember, it is your job to use Juni's coordinates and find the SNZ 100. You have to trust us to take care of the enemy."

"Of course, I do," Carmen said.

"And you have to figure out how to dismantle this device," Dad said seriously.

"Check," Carmen said.

"*But* you should not touch the SNZ 100," Dad added. "As heavily electrified as this island is, I'm sure the SNZ 100 has enough power to zap you to Timbuktu."

"Got it," Carmen said. But by now, her voice was a little shaky. And her stomach was flopping around like a brute on the verge of a sneeze.

"You can do it, Carmen," Juni said. He reached down from his perch at the top of the palm tree and patted his sister on the shoulder.

"Thanks," Carmen squeaked. She gazed up and down the palm tree's trunk at her brother's eyes, her mom's smiling face, her dad's steely jaw.

And suddenly, all the butterflies were banished from her stomach.

"Okay," she announced. "I'm ready."

"Me, too!" Juni said.

"Ready!" Mom agreed.

"Here we go!" Dad added.

With some awkward stretches, the Cortezes

slapped their hands on top of one another until they'd made a sizable stack. Then they reached for their shoelaces and gave them a yank.

Fwooooom! Their rocket shoes burst into life.

Carmen made the first move. Waving good-bye to her parents and Juni, she shot through the palm tree's leaves. Then she flew straight toward the cluster of robotic parrots.

"Polly want a Cortez?" she teased. She did a loop-de-loop around one parrot and zipped beneath the sharp claws of another.

The parrots quickly began squawking and snapping at Carmen. But she was too quick. She darted out in front of them. Then she began flying toward the palm tree where her family was hiding.

"Catch me if you can," Carmen cried. She zoomed past the tree.

The instant Carmen passed by, Juni and Mom darted *out* of the tree. They pulled behind them a giant net that they'd woven from their palm tree's stringy bark. Juni flew up and Mom flew down. Dad gripped the other end of the net from his perch in the tree. Then all three spies pulled on the net until it was stretched taut—completely blocking the robot parrots' path.

SQUAAAAAWWWWKKK!

The birds crashed into the net, one after another, smashing into one another with a tremendous crunch. When the last parrot had tumbled into their trap, the spies let go. The pile of birds tumbled to the jungle floor, and exploded in a giant fireball.

"Whoa!" Juni cried. He and his parents flew into the sky and out of harm's way. They gazed across the treetops at Carmen, who was hovering anxiously in the air nearby.

"We're fine!" Dad whispered to her through his spy watch's walkie-talkie. "Now get to the SNZ 100 as fast as you can. You can do it, Carmen!"

"See you soon!" Carmen's voice said through the spy watch. "Over!"

With that, Carmen began to zoom across the island to the clearing.

Of course, Sinus's weaponry wasn't going to make it easy for her. As she flew, hundreds of palm trees began shooting explosive coconuts at her. Carmen dodged, weaved, and flipped out of the way. But that wasn't good enough for Gregorio Cortez.

"She may be an international superspy," he growled "but she's still my daughter! I can't just stand by and watch this!"

Dad yanked something out of his vest pocket. It

was a glass test tube stopped up by a cork.

"Uncle Machete's firebeans!" Juni said as he hovered nearby.

"*Si!*" Dad said resolutely. He flipped the tube's cork away with his thumbnail. Then he poured every last bean into his mouth.

"Whoa!" Juni said, turning to his mother with wide eyes. "Those beans are superspicy!"

"Did I ever tell you that your Dad won a chili-eating contest on our honeymoon in Mexico?" Mom replied. "No *problemo*!"

She was right. Dad flew right into the swarm of exploding coconuts. He was spitting mad—literally. He began shooting flames from his mouth, intercepting every coconut bomb he saw with a poof of fire. The coconuts exploded in midair.

Finally, the trees were out of coconut bombs, Dad was out of firebeans, and Carmen had made it through the firefight.

Of course, that's when the volcano began rumbling anew. Just as Carmen was about to fly past it, it spewed a great geyser of green acid.

Carmen was blocked! She stopped in midair and hesitated.

Mom, Dad, and Juni began to fly to her aid. As he zinged through the air, Dad pulled a bottle of white, chalky liquid out of his vest pocket.

"Ay, those spicy firebeans gave me heartburn," he complained. He took a big swig from the bottle. But before he could return it to his pocket, Juni had grabbed it.

"Heartburn medicine!" Juni said. "It has sodium bicarbonate in it. And every spy knows . . ."

"Sodium bicarbonate neutralizes acid!" Mom said. "Juni, you did your homework!"

"But we need a solution to mix it with," Dad pointed out. "This little bottle isn't enough for that big volcano."

"I'm thinking milk shake," Juni said, with a nod.

"Juni, I promise, we'll get you a snack later," Mom said distractedly. "But this is no time for the munchies."

"No, Mom," Juni said. "A *coconut* milk shake!"

"Of course!" Mom cried. "You really *did* do your homework!"

"Will you please remember that when my report card comes next week?" Juni said.

The three spies began zipping from palm tree to palm tree. They plucked every nonexplosive coconut they saw. Then Juni whipped his inflatable Sooper Salad Bowl out of his utility belt. With the touch of a button, the tiny, red bowl filled with air until it was the size of a small barrel. Juni held it as his parents quickly used their laser knives to cut dozens of coconuts in half. They emptied the nuts' thick, sweet milk into the bowl. Then Dad added his heartburn medicine.

And finally, the three Cortezes headed for the volcano. They held the big bowl of liquid between them, making sure not to spill a drop.

"This is going to take some bravery!" Dad said, as they approached the volcano.

"And speed!" Mom said.

"And good aim!" Juni added.

Gritting their teeth, the spies flew directly over the shuddering volcano. Just as they did, a spurt of acid shot out of its mouth. The acid was heading straight for them!

"Pour!" Dad ordered. Together, Mom, Dad, and Juni flung their concoction at the plume of acid. It made a direct hit! By the time the acid hit the family, it had been entirely neutralized. It was as harmless as water.

And when the remaining coconut milk poured into the volcano, the acid eruption halted altogether.

"Yes!" Juni yelled. He whirled around in midair and called to his sister.

"You're clear!" he said. "Go to the SNZ 100."

Carmen zipped over the dormant volcano and headed for the clearing, with her family right behind her.

When they finally reached their goal, they screeched to a halt in midair. Then they hovered, gaping in disbelief.

"Of course," Carmen whispered as she stared at the gigantic SNZ 100. "What else would make a 'big sneeze'?"

The SNZ 100 was a 200-foot-tall—nose. Constructed of steel and giant bolts, the device had a satellite dish positioned in each nostril and a cockpit on the bridge. And sitting inside the cockpit, of course, was Sinus. He was just waiting for his scientists in the Ol-Factory to move the SNZ 100 into position. Then he would hit the button that would sneeze into space the biggest computer virus the world had ever seen.

Unless, of course, the Cortezes could beat the big nose before it was locked into position.

There was only one thing standing in their way. Make that one girl. She was floating before them, wearing jet shoes of her own—Maya Sinclair!

CHAPTER 15

Carmen hovered in the air a few feet in front of her parents and brother. She was in a face-off with her ex-friend—Maya. The two glared at each other venemously. And neither girl was going to budge an inch.

Out of the corner of her eye, Carmen saw Juni's jet shoes give a little spurt of fire. She knew he was itching to join the battle against her traitorous friend. Mom and Dad surely felt the same way.

But Carmen turned to them and held up her hand.

"This is my fight," she told them. Respectfully, Mom, Dad, and Juni nodded and hung back. Then Carmen turned back to Maya.

"So, we meet again," she said. Her voice shook with anger.

"Indeed," Maya said in her clipped British accent. "You know I can't let you get to the SNZ 100, Carmen."

"And you know I *will* get to it, Maya," Carmen

replied. "And, hmmm, over the course of our friendship, *I've* told the truth. And y*ou've* lied through your teeth. So, I would be inclined to believe . . . me."

Carmen crossed her arms over her chest and nodded defiantly. Then she braced herself for a sarcastic comeback.

But instead of hurling an insult at Carmen, Maya did something shocking.

She started to cry.

She hung her head in shame. Her shoulders heaved with big, wet sobs.

"You're right, you're right," Maya said. "I've been a big fat liar. I abused your trust and—I'm so sorry!"

Maya looked up at Carmen with wan, teary eyes.

"But, Carmen," she said. "You have no idea what it's like, growing up with no parents to love you. You have the most wonderful family. I was just trying to be a part of it."

Carmen blinked at Maya in surprise. She glanced at Mom, Dad, and Juni—who were still floating nearby—and wondered what life would be like without them. The idea was so painful, she couldn't even fathom it.

Carmen turned back to Maya.

She squinted at the sobbing girl.

Juni's fists trembled, and he held his breath.

Their parents gave each other concerned glances.

And Maya pitifully wiped a tear from her eye.

Was Carmen hesitating? Was she going to let Maya—and Sinus—win?

At last, Carmen broke the silence.

"Maya," she said, quietly. "You're clearly upset."

Uh-oh, Juni thought. She's caving!

"And, I have to add," Carmen said slowly, "with all that crying, your makeup's a mess."

Huh? Juni thought.

"Let me help you powder your nose," Carmen offered. She reached into her pocket and pulled out a small, silver compact. When she flipped the makeup case open, a giant, fuzzy, glowing powder puff sproinged out.

Maya's eyes widened.

"No!" she cried. But Carmen was too quick for her. She lunged at Maya with the enormous puff and blew a cloud of powder into the traitor's face.

When Carmen pulled the puff away, Maya's eyes were red and her nose was redder. Her neck and hands instantly broke out in hives. Maya began scratching them frantically. Between scratches, she sneezed.

And sneezed and sneezed and sneezed.

In a few seconds, Maya was a weak, quivering bundle of allergies. She was utterly defenseless. Carmen grabbed her easily, slapped some hand-cuffs on her, and flew her down to the ground. Then she used her vest cable to tie the sneezing, sniffling double agent to a nonshocking tree.

"You will—*ahhhh-CHOO*—never get—*snorfle*—away with this," Maya said. She sneered at Carmen with her red and watery eyes.

"Uh-huh," Carmen said dryly. "Go on, Maya. Tell *another* lie. I dare you."

Then she turned on her heel and walked over to her family, who'd just landed behind her.

"I totally thought you were going to believe Maya's sob story," Juni said. He jumped up and down with excitement.

"Please," Carmen said. "I've learned my lesson. Never trust a double agent. *Except*, of course, when she gives you some of her makeup gadgets."

Carmen stuffed her huge powder puff back into the compact with a grin.

"What *is* that?" Juni asked, taking the compact from his sister.

"A Pollen Powder Puff," Carmen said casually. "During one of our 'heart-to-heart' chats, Maya just happened to mention to me that she's got mega-allergies. I used that information against her. Just like she tried to use my feelings for my family against me."

"You're a good spy, honey," Mom said. "But you're an even better daughter."

But this was no time for mushy stuff. Maya might have been out of the way, but Sinus was still manning the SNZ 100.

CHUNK! Whirrrrrrrrr.

And it had just sprung to life! The giant nose was slowly turning and angling toward the sky. A few more minutes and it would be in position to knock out every satellite in outer space!

Carmen and Juni looked at each other and squared their shoulders.

"Sinus is toast," Carmen declared.

The Spy Kids reached down and tugged on their bootlaces.

But instead of spitting fire, their jet shoes sputtered, sizzled, and sighed. And then—they completely died.

"Of all the times for our jet shoes to run out of fuel!" Juni said. "We have to get to Sinus before he can hit that button! But there's no time to climb up that monstrous nose."

Carmen squinted up at the SNZ 100's cockpit. Then her eyes lit up.

"Actually," she announced, "we won't have to. Mom, you've got the laptop with the wireless modem, don't you?"

"Check," Mom said, whipping the slim computer out of her backpack. "All booted up."

"Excellent," Carmen said. She sat on the ground and snapped the computer open. Then she began typing so fast, her fingers blurred.

"What's she doing?" Juni asked his parents.

"Shhh," Dad replied. "I've never seen Carmen hack with such intensity. This is going to be verrrry interesting."

"I'm in!" Carmen announced, suddenly. "I've hacked into the cockpit's audio output."

She leaned over the computer's microphone and pushed one last button.

"Ahem, excuse me, Sinus?" she said.

"What? Who said that?" wheezed Sinus's voice in the laptop's speaker. The Cortezes looked up at and saw the skinny dictator spot them. He shook his fist at them. Then he impatiently tapped his fingers on the cockpit's control panel. The SNZ 100 was still whirring into place. He couldn't activate the Big Sneeze until it was in the proper position to zap the satellites.

"Sinus," Carmen said, "Before you destroy every satellite in outer space and take over the world, could I just say one thing?"

"Oh, you think I'll fall for that one again?" Sinus whined. "Not a chance!"

I thought you'd say that," Carmen said, with a sly smile. "All right, then. Have it your way. No words."

Instead, Carmen reached into her vest pocket and pulled out a little red box with a small dial on it.

"It's Maya's high-frequency device!" Juni whispered to his parents.

"Let's see," Carmen whispered. "If eight twenty-five to the tenth power paralyzes gelatinous invertebrates, what will it take to conquer a spineless mad doctor?"

Carmen plugged the high-frequency device into the computer's audio-output system. That meant only Sinus—in his speaker-filled cockpit—would be able to hear the high-pitched shrieking of the little red box.

All Carmen had to do was spin the dial to just the correct frequency.

"I'm thinking, eighteen fifty to the fifth power?" she said to Juni. "What do you say?"

"Go for it," Juni agreed.

Carmen spun the dial.

Then the Cortezes gazed up at the cockpit of the SNZ 100.

They saw Sinus clap his spidery hands over his ears. He swayed back and forth in pain. He screamed in agony. And finally, he reached out and smashed a few buttons.

The giant nose de-electrified with a sizzling sound. Then, an inflatable escape ramp unfurled from the cockpit. It unrolled down the length of the giant nose and began to puff up with air. When the long slide was inflated, Sinus opened the cockpit's door and tumbled outside. Carmen quickly turned off the high-frequency device as the screaming Sinus slithered down the slide. He landed in a heap at the bottom.

The Cortezes stepped toward the sniveling supervillain. But before they could reach him, Sinus used his last ounce of strength to pull out something from behind his back.

It was a weapon! A sprayer attached to a jar of bubbling green liquid.

"You will *not* foil my evil plan," Sinus rasped. "You thought my gas-passers were powerful? Well, you haven't smelled a stench until you've sucked up some of this stuff. Prepare to sniff yourselves into a stupor, Cortezes!"

As Sinus's trembly finger fumbled with the sprayer, Juni gazed at the mad doctor. He homed in on his milky skin and his big, red, drippy nose. Then he glanced at his parents and Carmen.

"I got this one," Juni said. He reached into the pocket where he'd stashed Carmen's Pollen Powder Puff. He pulled the enormous, yellow pom-pom from the compact. Then he gently blew a puff of pollen in Sinus's direction.

"What are you doing?" Sinus demanded. "There's no need to powder your nose now, my boy. Soon, you'll wish you were born *without* a nose. You'll be bathed in the world's smelliest ga . . . ga . . . *gaaaahhh-choooo!*"

The moment the first specks of pollen reached Sinus's huge, quivery sniffer, he began to sneeze. And tremble. And sniffle. And shake.

Juni nodded triumphantly.

"I had a hunch that Sinus had allergies, too," he said. Mom and Dad rushed over to the skinny, sniveling villain. It took almost no effort to overpower him. They dragged him over to the still sneezing Maya. Then they handcuffed the two baddies to each other.

"Hey," Carmen said, eyeing the evildoers' drippy noses and bloodshot eyes. "I think Maya got her wish. I'm beginning to see a family resemblance here!"

"And you know what they say," Juni said. "Nothing brings a family closer than close quarters. Like prison cells."

"Oh, is that what they say?" Mom said. She and Dad had sauntered over to their kids. "I thought it was a steady supply of snacks."

With that, Mom pulled two big chocolate bars out of her spy vest and presented them to her hungry children. Juni rolled his eyes in rapture and immediately took an enormous bite.

Over their heads, a fleet of OSS helicopters suddenly appeared. They'd arrived to take Sinus, Maya, and all of Mortille's evil scientists and brutes into custody, then dismantle the evil SNZ 100.

The Cortezes had accomplished their mission. It was time to go home.

"You know, Mom," Carmen said as the spy family headed down the jungle trail toward their drill sub. "Maya *was* right about one thing."

"Really?" Mom said with wide eyes. "What was that?"

"As international superspy parents go, you and Dad," Carmen admitted, "are pretty cool."